Party at Castle Grof

The Tower and The Eye, Volume 2

Kira Morgana

Published by Teigr Books, 2024.

PARTY AT CASTLE GROF

First edition. June 30, 2024.

Copyright © 2024 Kira Morgana.

ISBN: 979-8227069146

Written by Kira Morgana.

Table of Contents

This one is dedicated to the people who inspired the initial encounter told within these pages... they know who they are.

Prologue

High in the Heart Mountains stands a Tower. The rough-cut basalt walls grow from the forbidding landscape and form a shape reminiscent of a giant ossified tree. The dark red glow discharged from the encircling windows into the predawn darkness is the only sign that someone is home...

From his throne, Aracan Katuvana surveyed the room around him, his hood obscuring his face. A suit of black armour hung on a stand to one side, a sinister helm with a mottled gold crown riveted to the brow on a table beside it. On the weapon stand next to the table, a massive double-handed sword and black steel mace glittered in the candlelight.

Clapping his hands, the Aracan summoned an ancient, gnarled Goblin wearing a black tabard.

The goblin bowed to the red and black robed figure on the tarnished throne and turned to a pedestal where a large, polished basalt Jar with a carving of a monocular face on the front rested.

The eye opened; an iris like green swirling mist regarded the goblin.

"Well? I can't see what is going on from here, Stupid."

The Goblin bowed again, moved behind the pedestal and picked the Jar up.

"Good Morrow, Lord," the Jar said as the Goblin brought it around to face Aracan Katuvana. "What is your plan for this fine day?"

Rising, the Aracan strode to the western windows, his robes flowing softly around him. The Goblin scurried behind, carrying the Jar.

Tapping a symbol engraved into the windowsill, Katuvana brought up the image of a large city amongst foothills, cradled on one side by red rock and on the other by the granite.

The Jar blinked and pursed its lips.

"If I do not miss my guess that is Valdez, the capital city of Valdier. What do you wish to know?"

Katuvana grunted. The Jar looked up at the Goblin.

"Stupid, put me down and bring volume three of the Valdier text."

The goblin put the Jar on a plinth next to the window, turned and left the room, his joints creaking. He returned with a massive book, which he placed on a reading stand beside the Jar.

"Page eight hundred and three, Stupid." The Jar watched as the goblin turned the pages, counting silently. When he stopped turning the pages, the Jar ran its eye over the text quickly. "Very well Lord, here is the overview of Valdier: Home to a valiant and brave people who fight for what they believe in but have sharp tempers and sharper swords." The Jar let out a bark of a laugh. "Sounds like they'd make excellent additions to your army, but their sense of honour would cause a few problems."

The Aracan Katuvana folded his arms, a growling sound emerging from under the hood.

"There are very few from that city in our ranks, my Lord. I take it that you would like to cause some chaos there?" The Jar seemed relieved when the Aracan Katuvana gave a sharp nod. "Where do you wish to start?"

Katuvana pressed a second icon and the view zoomed into the north side of the city, centring on a large building on one side of a market square.

"Ah, the Mountain's Shadow Tavern, plenty of potential entertainment here. Is there anyone in particular within that you would like to use?" The Jar smiled as the Aracan indicated a huge barbarian warrior with dark shaggy hair, unkempt beard and moustache, sitting outside. His rust and mud speckled breastplate and greaves suggested that he had recently travelled a long distance. The huge pack on the floor beside him backed that impression up, as did the thick coating of mud on his boots.

The warrior had a large tankard of ale in one hand and a bread roll in the other. Across from him, a mage in the grey robes of neutrality, picked at a plate of cheese and bread in front of him. His exhausted looking narrow face and pale skin with patches of sunburn told the watchers that he also had been on a journey. His gold wire frame eyeglasses had been repaired more than once and cracks were spidering across one of the lenses.

"An excellent choice, Lord, they both look as if they have much potential. Which human would you like to play with?"

The Aracan Katuvana snapped his fingers and the view focused on the warrior.

The Jar cackled.

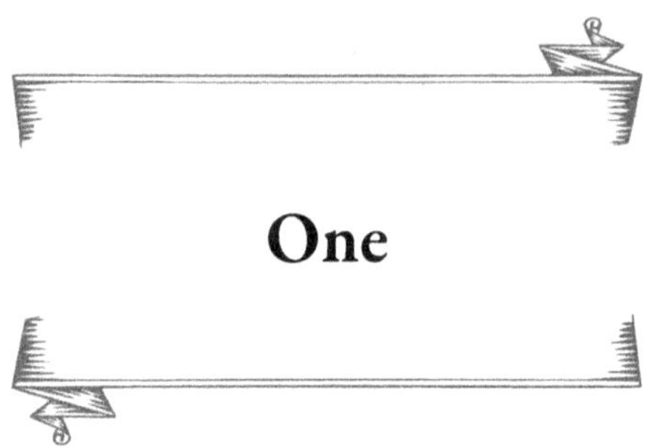

One

A fly swooped past Grald's eyes, buzzing.

"What was that?" he muttered. The fly looped around and landed on his nose; his eyes crossed to focus on the creature and raised his free hand

"Stay right there you," he said and aimed a slap at it and then cursed as it took off again and he hit his own face. "Whoops." He blinked rapidly to uncross his eyes, "Ow. Bloody bug."

"What was what?" his undernourished companion asked, looking up from his plate as he spread soft cheese on a hunk of bread.

"Something buzzed me and now I feel odd," Grald mumbled, trying to work out what he'd done to himself. He peered at the hand he'd hit himself with, then peered into his tankard.

"You always feel odd drinking Wingdangs. Why don't you try the local mead?" the other man said.

"You may have it there, Shilir. Ho, bar wench." Grald waved at one of the girls who were delivering food and drink to a nearby table, momentarily forgetting the stein of Wizard Wingdangs Original Ale in that hand. It slopped over the side and splashed all over the dwarf sitting at the next table.

"What do ye think ye're doing, Laddie!" The dwarf erupted out of his seat, the sweet, caramel-smelling ale dripping from the horns on his helm and soaking into his thick beard.

"I'm sorry sir, it was an accident; he didn't mean anything by it." Shilir got up and pushed between Grald and the dwarf.

"A lad that big never does things by accident, mage," the dwarf said.

"Believe me, in the whole time I have known him, Grald has done a lot of things by accident," Shilir essayed a nervous grin.

"Shilir, get out of the way; let me deal with this half-pint drinker." Grald surged forward and looked surprised when Shilir pushed him back. He stumbled, caught himself against the table and bit his tongue. "Ow."

"Half-Pint drinker, ye say? I'll have ye're ears for that, ya overgrown lout." The dwarf threw Shilir aside and launched himself at the barbarian.

Scrambling up from the ruins of the bench he had landed on, Shilir almost knocked someone in white robes flying. Elbowing his way through the gathering crowd he dashed into the common room and ran headlong into the long wooden bar.

"Help, my companion won't be able to defend himself. Help him!" he said, trying to recover his breath.

The Tavern Keeper glanced out at the fight going on outside and shook his head, rolling his eyes. "I hope he can pay for the damage."

Shilir groaned and turned to the half-elf beside him. "Please?"

"Which one is your friend?" the half-elf asked, looking over at the fight.

"Grald the Barbarian." Shilir started to panic and grabbed the half-elf's arm.

"The big guy? You're worried about the dwarf beating him up. He looks like he can handle himself," the half-elf laughed.

"You don't understand. He's been drinking Wizard Wingdangs Original Ale... something in it weakens him to the point where a kitten could maim him with one swat of its tail; even a feather could knock him over. Please help him."

"Why should we help your friend? I don't even know why the fight started." A feminine voice floated over his shoulder. Shilir turned to see the white robed mage he had bumped into.

"You took your time, Ariana," the half-elf said, without turning round.

"The Guild wanted to hear my report. It took a little while," Ariana replied, irritation etching her elegant face.

"If it had taken any longer, you'd have been peeling me up off the floor."

"Well, if you didn't drink human ale, Aranok, you wouldn't need my hangover potion." The mage looked over at the fight in the corner. "The barbarian does seem to be coming off worse in his fight with the dwarf."

Shilir looked at Ariana hopefully. "Can you help?"

"I used most of my mana up on illusions during my report. Sorry, Brother." She shook her head. "I haven't replenished my mana potions yet." Ariana tilted her head to one side and smiled at Shilir. "Unless you have a spare one?"

Shilir groaned. "I haven't restocked yet either. Grald and I only arrived this morning."

Grald was starting to wonder if responding to the dwarf had been a bad idea. An insistent trickle of blood from a cut on his forehead interfered with his vision, dripping through his thick eyebrows.

"How about we talk about this?" he asked, wiping his eyes again.

The dwarf growled and slammed a fist into Grald's chest. Grald's breath whooshed out of his body, and he staggered back.

"Maybe not then," he wheezed, grabbing the dwarf by his chest plate and attempting to drop kick him through the window. Unfortunately, his befuddled body barely allowed him to lift the dwarf off the ground.

The dwarf leaned back in his grip, planted a foot into Grald's stomach and used the other one to kick at his nose. Grald lurched backward, sat down hard on a bench and dropped the dwarf at the same time.

The dwarf landed on his chest and took the opportunity to punch Grald in the mouth. The bench tipped from the movement, sending the labourer sitting on the other end flying through the air into the window and spilling both Grald and the dwarf onto the straw strewn cobbles.

The window smashed as the labourer flew through it and landed on a table. The occupants of the table, a group of bakers having their lunchtime game of cards, swore as the cards and coins scattered under the man's landing.

The table broke, all the tankards on it tipped over and the bakers left trying to gather up their coppers and piled onto the unfortunate labourer.

"I'll be adding that window and the furniture to your friend's bill." The Tavern Keeper carried on polishing his tankards calmly.

Shilir groaned.

Sighing, Aranok pulled a field tip arrow out of his quiver and twisted on his stool to face the fight. The crowd around the bar drew back as he sighted along it, pulled his arm back, and threw it like a miniature javelin.

Grald stood up and stared in shock at the result of his near miss with a dwarven boot.

"Did I do that?" he murmured, swaying a little as the dwarf tried to trip him up.

Something brushed past his ear, so he turned to see what it was. Tripping over his own feet, Grald fell over and landed on the next table. The boards splintered under his weight and as Grald hit the floor, he knocked himself senseless on his own mace.

"Hah! That's what ye get for spilling ale on Avinger McCraken!" The dwarf laughed and kicked Grald squarely in the balls. Then he stomped away, shouting, "I ain't standing for that kind o'treatment. I'm gonna get the Watch!"

"Oh great, now I have to try and pick him up again. I put my back out for a week last time I did that; he weighs as much as a tun of beer. I don't suppose that you could give me a hand?" Shilir groaned.

"Yeah, all right," Aranok said, handing his bow and quiver to Ariana before following Shilir out to the prone barbarian.

Ariana took their things to a free table, while between them the skinny mage and the half-elven ranger half-dragged, half-carried, the eight-foot slab of muscle into the tavern and onto the bench across from her.

"You got one of those hangover potions?" Aranok waved a hand at his companion.

She sighed and rummaged in her bag.

"Here, pour this down his throat." Ariana handed Shilir a tiny vial with a red liquid in it. "It takes about three minutes to clear the alcohol's effects."

Shilir fed Grald the potion.

"I'd better go and pay the Tavern Keeper for the damage. Can I get you a drink to show my thanks?" He pulled out his money pouch as he stood up.

"Galivorn Firewater, please," Aranok said, dropping onto a stool beside Ariana.

"Aleth Ale for me, please," Ariana smiled at the skinny mage, who smiled back hesitantly.

Aranok grimaced at his sister's effect on men. "Ariana, stop that!"

She laughed. "You stop with the protective brother thing then."

"Be careful around my sister, Mage. She had an even half dozen men of all sorts of races chasing her the last time I looked." Aranok rolled his eyes.

Shilir blushed. "Ah. Can you stay here and keep an eye on my friend, please. I'll, um, be back in a jiffy." He wandered off in the direction of the bar.

Aranok waved a hand. "Will do."

"Aranok, you're just too soft hearted, do you know that? We should be restocking for our trip home," Ariana said, rummaging in her cloak pockets as the other mage disappeared into the crowd.

"I know," the Ranger grunted. "It comes from my mother's half. We can wait a couple of hours before we set out." Settling his back against the wall, Aranok yawned and closed his eyes.

"No falling asleep on me, Aranok, or I'll pour your drink over you to wake you up," Ariana warned him.

Aranok stuck his tongue out at her without opening his eyes.

"I swear you're the most childish half-elf I have ever met," his sister sighed. "Liana will never say yes if you don't grow up soon."

"She'll say yes. I know she will," the ranger grunted. "We grew up together, I know her better than I know you."

"Only because you two were born a hundred or so years before me." Ariana shook her head. "And you're still acting like you're a child of fifty, not an adult of a hundred and ninety-two."

The tavern door flew open, forestalling Aranok's rejoinder and Avinger McCraken stormed back into the common room, followed by a full squad of the City Watch.

"Where is he, McCraken?" the officer asked in a noble accent, as he absently balled a soft cloth from a belt pouch and buffed the gilded vambrace protecting his left forearm.

The dwarf scanned the room, and spotted Grald rising groggily from the bench as the potion finished its work. The dwarf yelled and pointed at Grald.

"There! That's the bugger who assaulted me, Officer! See, he's sitting with his friends now!"

"Right then." The Officer strode over to the table, tucking the soft cloth away. "I arrest all of you in the name of King Groilin who, as all who value their lives know, is King of Valdir. The charges facing you are: one count of assault; two counts of causing an affray and one count of damaging private property."

"What?" Ariana blinked.

"Boys, bring them down to the Watch House!" The Officer snapped his fingers and three of the burly guards grabbed Aranok.

"Hang on a minute, I broke up the fight, I didn't start it. The dwarf did," Aranok protested, pulling away from the men, who had almost lifted him from his stool.

The dwarf growled. "The Barbarian was th'one who emptied his flagon on me."

"And I stopped him from beating you senseless. I had nothing to do with what he did." The guards grabbed his arms. He flung them off again. "Leave me alone."

"Doesn't matter who did what; you're coming with us. If in the course of our investigations, we discover your story is true, then we'll let you out. It shouldn't take more than a couple of months," the officer replied, waving a lazy hand in greeting at the Tavern Keeper.

Another couple of men grabbed Grald, slinging the groaning barbarian between them.

"You're joking. Ask the mage at the bar, he's the one who asked us to break it up! Hoi, magic boy; sort this out!" Aranok shouted at Shilir, who he could just see at the bar.

Ariana was politely, if firmly, urged out of her seat by another pair of guards.

"A couple of months? That's ridiculous," she declared, her outrage making her hands glow with suppressed power.

The officer frowned. "Now you watch yourself, Miss. We pride ourselves as being fair on prisoners and if you do something rash, I may be forced to do something you may come to regret."

"Shilir?" Grald called out weakly "What's going on?"

Shilir turned round and his eyes widened.

"Sweet Fiörna!" He started struggling through the crowd calling out to the barbarian, "I'll sort this out, Grald. Just don't do anything foolish."

Aranok continued to protest their innocence and some of the Tavern's other customers took up the cry on his behalf.

"Leave them alone!"

"They didn't do anything!"

The Watch dragged Grald, Ariana and Aranok out of the tavern.

Many of the drinkers from the tavern boiled out onto the street, following the watchmen. Outside, the people on the street swelled the group around the prisoners, gawking at the show.

"Bloody Dwarves, they always start fights in Valdez, should be banned," one man yelled at the Watch Captain, who ignored the comment.

"How dare ye blame the Dwarves? Blame the humans, they're a contentious lot!" Avinger howled with rage and ploughed into the crowd toward the speaker, an elf wearing a mercenary uniform.

A few people threw tomatoes snatched up from a nearby stall, the fruit splattering on the back plates of the guards holding Ariana.

"Hey." The mage shrieked as the juice splashed onto her white robes. "Have you any idea how hard it is to get tomato juice out of white wool?"

The two guards dropped her arms and backed away, hands held palm up toward her.

"It wasn't us, lady..." one of them said.

"Fancy manhandling a gentlewoman like that," a female voice said from the crowd. "How dare they? Let her go."

Several other women chimed in and there was a surge toward Ariana as the women endeavoured to free her. Her guards stopped trying to catch hold of her again and concentrated on stopping the crowd from pulling Ariana away from them.

A tall, slim dark skinned elf, her face hidden in the shadow of her cloak's hood slipped into the edges of the crowd surrounding the kerfuffle. Those two can't seem to go anywhere without getting into trouble. *Maybe I should help them out of this one...* She raised one hand.

As the Captain turned to deal with the threatening riot, there was a shout from a fair way behind them. A bright light whooshed overhead to impact against a nearby Fishmongers cart. There was a soft hissing noise and anyone who understood what it was headed for the floor.

Satisfied, Erendell slid away again and sought shelter beside a leatherworker's stall, crouching down. Everyone else carried on as they were; fighting, yelling and generally causing trouble.

The cart exploded, showering everyone nearby in fish. The guards cursed but hung onto Aranok. Ariana's guards frowned, looking at her.

"It wasn't me," she told them. "My mana is all out, the trick with my hands is genetic."

A huge salmon thwacked into Grald's face, bringing him fully awake.

"What in all the Gods names is goin' on?" he hollered and with a few well-placed thumps managed to get free.

The crowd surrounding them cheered.

"Freedom for barbarians," someone yelled. "No more using us as mercenaries!"

The officer swung round, panic covering his face and he completely turned his back on the crowd as he saw Grald knock his guards out. "Grab the Barbarian!"

"Get ready!" a voice called from the back of the crowd.

Ariana frowned. *That voice sounds familiar.*

Another light ball flew over the top of the throng to hit the pompous officer on the back of the head and splintered into a thousand shimmering sparks. The officer groaned and slumped to the ground.

"Who did that?" the Officer's second in command yelled.

"I think he went that way," a woman wearing a seamstress' wrap said. She pointed down the street toward the main market.

"Thank you, ma'am." The watchman saluted her and frowned. "We'd better catch whoever it was, lads. Two of you get the captain and take him back to the watch house."

"What about these three?" one of the patrol asked.

The Lieutenant sighed and turned to Aranok.

"As I've never seen you in the city before and this is likely your first offence in Valdez, I'll let you go with a caution; you're not to cause any more trouble in the city or I will personally slam you in the cells."

Aranok and Ariana nodded their thanks. Dragging Grald away from his tussle with the guards, the three of them took advantage of the confusion to retrieve their belongings from the tavern, before following Grald over to a nearby alley.

Erendell dissolved the illusion of the seamstress she'd wrapped around herself and watched the little group disappear down the alley. *This can't be the cause of this damned itch in my bones. Something a bit bigger than a barroom brawl is afoot here and those two are going to get themselves killed unless I tag along.*

"Great. Now we can't go back there," Ariana groused, adjusting one of the straps on her satchel.

"We'll just have to find somewhere else for tonight." Aranok didn't seem concerned.

"Look, I'm sorry about all that," Grald said. "Shilir's pulled me out of a few scrapes since he turned up on my doorstep in Jinra Village, but I've never got anyone else in trouble before."

"That's all right," Ariana smiled at the big barbarian.

"If you come from Jinra Village, what on earth are you doing in Valdez?" Aranok asked, as he attached his quiver to his belt.

"Shilir would be the best one to ask about that." Grald looked around and spotted the skinny mage across the street. "There he is. Let's go and talk to him."

They crossed to another alley where Shilir waited. In the distance, they could hear the shouts and whistles of the Watch.

"What in Lady Hel's name was that all about?" Aranok fumed at the mage. "Why didn't you help us? You said this was your home town."

"I'm sorry. My employer often sorts things like that out for me. That's why I said for you to hang on." Shilir apologised as he led them down the alley. "Grald is a peaceable man, but anyone smaller than him seems to get upset with him, especially when he's drunk. Why he drinks Windang's is beyond me, especially when he knows the effect it has on him, but..." and he shrugged holding his hands out palm up.

Grald looked embarrassed. "Sorry, Shilir."

"So, what are you two doing in Valdez? I wasn't aware that the Guild of Mages had any elven representatives." The mage sat himself on a crate.

"I'm not Elven. I'm human." Ariana crossed her arms.

"But you are from Alethdariel?" The other mage looked slightly worried. "I'm sure I heard you mention the Heir to the Alethdariel throne earlier."

"How did you hear that? I didn't speak that loudly." Aranok's brows lowered. Ariana smacked him in the ribs, and he rubbed his side. "Ow, what did you do that for?"

She turned back to Shilir. "You were well away from us during that conversation. What gives you the right to listen in on us using a spell?"

"Um..." Shilir looked down at his feet. "I've had a tracking and listening spell on Grald ever since we went through Jirit, and he managed to get himself abducted by a group of Giranathian slavers. I just happened to overhear your conversation about Princess Liana and growing up together, that's all, I wasn't deliberately eavesdropping."

"Why are you interested in where we are from or what we are doing?" Aranok asked. "We just helped you out in a fight that wasn't ours."

"We were waiting for some friends of mine, but none of them have turned up." Grald looked worried. "They were taking the shortcut through the Heart Mountains from Jirshan."

"Dangerous route that one, it goes straight past Tower Lake," Aranok said.

"Well, there were four of them. A mage, a cleric and two warriors, it should have been safe enough." He sighed. "I said I would meet them here at the Mountain's Shadow and in theory they should have been here first. Only because Shilir insisted on going the long way round..." Grald looked at the mage who looked up at the sky and shrugged.

"That's all very well, but you haven't answered my question, Shilir. Why were you eavesdropping?" Ariana's hands began glowing again.

"We've been waiting for Grald's friends since early this morning. As they haven't turned up, I was trying to see if you'd be interested in a proposition." Shilir scooted backward as Ariana stalked toward him, her glowing hands clenched into fists.

"It's against Guild rules to use magic to eavesdrop in a public place, Shilir." She extended one hand, her index finger pointing at Shilir's long nose. "Why didn't you just ask?"

"I needed to know if you are trustworthy." Shilir leaned against the wall, eyes crossing as he kept his gaze on her finger. "Anyone who talks about Princess Liana in such familiar terms..." he flinched and fell off his crate as Aranok launched himself at him.

Ariana sighed and grabbed her brother. "Aranok, don't get carried away again."

"But..." Aranok let her pull him away from the trembling mage who had scrambled to hide behind Grald.

"I know. It's your duty. Behave yourself or do you want to end up in a cell?" Ariana swung back to glare at Shilir and Grald. "Now, tell us what in the Healing Lady's name you are going on about."

"Look. I'll be honest with you. Grald won't go into the Dungeon of Doom my employer found without a full party..."

Aranok blinked and scowled at the mage.

"A Dungeon of Doom?" Ariana looked troubled. "The Guild said something about that. Who is your employer that he can afford the Guild of Mages intervention?"

"Lord Harnez has the king's backing as well as a lot of money. There is something particular that the Guild wants from the Dungeon though." Shilir's eyes looked hunted. "That was how I got involved with the quest."

"Quest?" Aranok said.

"Shilir, let's take them to see Lord Harnez," Grald suggested. "He's the one who wants me to go into the Dungeon and he'd be the best one to explain exactly what is going on."

"Wonderful idea, Grald." Shilir's voice held a slight sneer. "Didn't think you had such intelligence in you."

Grald still recovering from the fight, didn't catch the second half of Shilir's comment and frowned. "What? Oh, never mind." He turned to Ariana. "Will you come to see Lord Harnez at least?"

She bit her bottom lip. We really ought to be restocking and getting back home. Mother will be getting worried. "I don't know. We'll have to talk it over."

"How much information do you need?" Shilir burst out. "You're adventurers, aren't you? This wouldn't be any different to what you do normally."

Aranok's eyes narrowed. "Actually, I'm Ariana's Mage Protector. We don't normally travel far from Alethdariel. If my sister wants to discuss with me whether or not we should even be talking to your employer, then I am not going to gainsay her. Besides, I don't like your tone."

Shilir threw up his hands and stalked away muttering.

Grald grinned. "For someone who came close to death on his last trip into a dungeon, he's not particularly cautious. I understand why you'd hesitate. We'll be over here when you come to your decision." He joined Shilir. "I'll make sure he doesn't eavesdrop this time."

Ariana turned her back on the barbarian and mage.

"Aranok, mother will be getting worried. We were only supposed to be bringing Lady Eliethor's report to the Mage's Guild, nothing more."

"The Dungeons of Doom are big trouble and if the Guild is trying to retrieve something from the treasure room of one, then the whole of Quargard could end up in danger." Aranok pulled himself upright.

"Aranok, those places have been quiet for at least a hundred years. I'm sure the Guild can handle any problems. They don't need us." Ariana could see logic wasn't swaying her brother. "Besides, Liana will be waiting for you. You have to get back to her."

"Liana would understand. Mother would understand and the Queen would expect us to get involved." Aranok raised an eyebrow at her. "What's the real reason you don't want to go?"

"I don't trust them. They've already brought us a great deal of trouble," she said, watching Grald and the mage with narrowed eyes.

"That brawl? I've been in worse during the Midwinter Festival at home." Her brother laid a gentle hand on one arm. "Let's go and hear what this Lord Harnez has to say. It would be a better plan based on more information anyway."

"Ok, fine. But I still don't trust them," Ariana muttered, rubbing the back of her arms. What is wrong with me? Normally I'd be as interested as Aranok. There's something wrong here; I can feel it.

They rejoined Grald and Shilir.

"We'll at least hear your employer out." Aranok said.

"Excellent. This way please." Shilir ushered them through the gate.

Erendell focused her keen hearing on the group. Dungeons of Doom? Now that sounds interesting. She slipped swiftly through the gate after them, staying close enough to hear what was going on. The mention of the involved Lord gave her pause. Maybe not. Aristocracy always means trouble. She leaned against a nearby wall and watched the other four. Dungeons of Doom or find a bar for a drink? Damn, they're moving again. I'd better catch up. Goddess knows what trouble they'll find themselves in next.

Shilir began striding off up the street towards the Palace. Grald followed him, Aranok keeping pace with the Jinran. Ariana had to move fast to keep up.

He led them to a fine house, just down the hill from the Palace of King Groilin. The extensive gardens had large shade trees bordering the paved path, providing welcome relief from the midsummer heat.

"Wait here please," Shilir said before disappearing into the house, leaving them on the front portico.

"Have you noticed that Shilir's got all business like?" Ariana whispered to Aranok.

The half-elf nodded. "My ear tips are tingling."

"That's not a good sign," Ariana said, poking him. "Let's go, before we get into something we can't get out of."

Aranok glanced at Grald, who was surreptitiously clearing his nose out with the one little finger of one hand and his ear with the index finger of other hand.

"All right, Sis. Don't poke my ribs like that, I bruise easily."

She snorted and covered her mouth to stop a giggle from escaping.

Grald rolled his eyes. "You two are like a couple of kids."

"I'm a half elf, we take a long time to mature and she's still a babe in arms in comparison." Aranok moved out of Ariana's reach as she jabbed one hand toward him again.

"I'm serious, Aranok. I have an increasingly bad feeling about this." Ariana lowered her voice and moved closer to him. "Let's get out of here."

He pulled a face. "Are you sure?"

She nodded.

He shrugged and hefted his bag. "Okay then."

Grald sighed mournfully. "You're going then? Just as I was beginning to get used to you, too."

Ariana looked at him. "I'm sorry, Grald..." she started, but before she could finish apologising and move away and head down the drive, Shilir reappeared.

"Come on through now," he said.

"Too late." Aranok smiled at her reassuringly when his sister's face dropped into annoyance. "It can't hurt to listen, Ariana."

With a sour expression on her face, Ariana followed the two men and the mage into the house.

Erendell sprinted up the path, but it was too late. "Damn." She grimaced and concentrated on getting her breath back. *What would you have said if you'd caught up with them anyway?* Her conscience berated her. *Aranok said he never wanted to see you again after the debacle in Reldheim.*

She straightened up and headed back toward the gates. *I'll catch them when they come back out and find out what's going on then.*

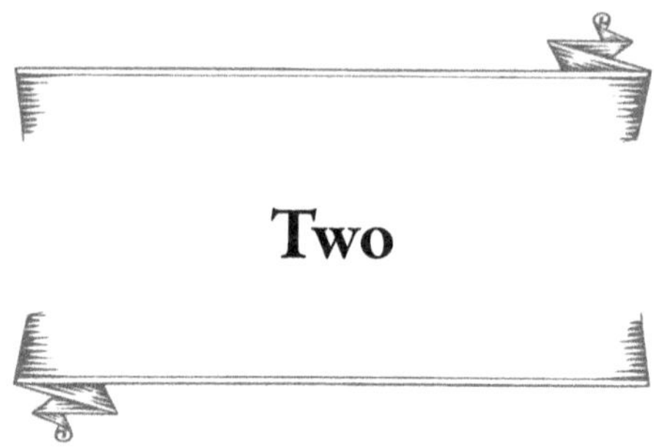

Two

S hilir led them into a large room. Hundreds of books lined the walls and a tall rack of scrolls stood between two stained glass windows depicting Tyr, the God of War, Battles and Honour, and Espilieth, Goddess of Magic and Healing, both deities shown in their human guises.

Despite the season, the room was quite cool. Next to the empty fireplace, a small shrine bore a porcelain statuette of Espilieth in white robes and a tiny brazier in front of the figure sent up a strong floral scent from the smouldering coals.

At least this lord is calling the Lady's aid down properly; that's an expensive rose incense from Franier he's burning. Ariana deeply inhaled the scent of roses in full bloom with approval.

Aranok smiled and shook his head at her dreamy sigh when she exhaled. Blushing at being caught in her appreciation, Ariana looked around.

At the opposite end of the room from the windows, a large dark wood desk squatted, covered with paper, parchments, books and scrolls. Behind the desk sat a tall, heavyset man with thinning brown hair, his eyes moving over an ancient looking scroll.

Shilir bowed. "Lord Harnez, I have brought the Warrior Grald as you requested. He has found two companions to accompany him. They have requested a briefing on the Quest."

Ariana looked annoyed at Shilir's assumption. Aranok elbowed her before she could say anything.

Lord Harnez looked up from the papers he was studying.

"Thank you, Shilir, you may go." Shilir left the room and Harnez stood up and moving to a position beside the solid, carved clay, three-dimensional map that occupied the centre of the room.

"This is Valdier." Harnez pointed to the map. He looked up when he realised no one had moved. "Come over here, please."

Grald, Aranok and Ariana moved over to stand around the map.

"Right," Harnez continued, "just outside of Valdez are the ruins of Castle Grof, once the ancestral home of the powerful Alizarin Family. Located in the centre of the ruins is an entrance to one of the Dungeons of Doom." "You are familiar with the Legend of The Tower and The Eye, are you not?"

No one said anything and he frowned. "The Tower and The Eye? Never heard of it," Aranok replied. Ariana blinked and looked at him. He sent her the barest tip of a wink.

What's he up to? Ariana inclined her head a little in response and remained quiet. I remember being told stories about the heroes of the Black War as a child; he's older than me, he should know more about it than just stories.

Grald started, "You've never heard of the Legend of the Tower and The Eye?" he asked, sounding shocked.

Lord Harnez frowned. "Where on earth do you come from? I thought everyone knew the legend."

Aranok opened his mouth, but before a word had been spoken, Harnez waved the question away. "No, forget I asked."

He picked up an outsized tome, flipping through to a double spread of pictures.

"I'll explain.

"According to the legend recorded by Scholar Shallin Val'din in the year three hundred A.T., the four kingdoms of Valdier, Galivor, Jinran and Franier were once ruled over by the evil Aracan Katuvana from the Black Tower in the centre of the Heart Mountains."

He turned the page to a map. "To enforce his will on the people of the kingdoms, the Aracan Katuvana created the Dungeons of Doom. The network of dungeons and tunnels was supposed to spread across each kingdom. All of the Dungeons connected to the Tower with secret tunnels that were built around a vein of precious metals and gems."

The lord pointed out each of the locations in the appropriate places on the clay map. "Reldheim, the land of the Dwarves and Alethdariel, the ancestral home of the Elves, were able to stave the Aracan off for some considerable time, but eventually he began to encroach into their lands.

"This precipitated an uprising from within Galivor, led by Ser Senith, a Paladin of Espilieth, aided heavily by the Dwarves and Elves. Over time the oppressed peoples of Valdier, Franier and Jinran joined the revolution."

Lord Harnez shut the book with a snap, making Ariana jump.

"The Aracan Katuvana was eventually overthrown by the combined effort of all the Kingdoms. They raided the Dungeons, found the underground passages and stormed the Black Tower. Sir Senith destroyed the Aracan Katuvana and freed the kingdoms to run their own lives.

"Over time the entrances to the Dungeons were lost, some demolished, some bricked up, their surrounding castles destroyed, and the areas made forbidden to enter. For humans, it has been so long since the Overthrow that all that is left are the ruins, the scholarly legend and a fairy tale told to children to make them behave themselves." Harnez stopped speaking and assessed his audience's condition.

Grald looked like he had fallen asleep on his feet and was even snoring lightly.

Ariana eyed the three-dimensional map closely, whispering to Aranok: "Is it just me, or is there a flag in Alethdin?" she pointed. "It's right next to the border of our home."

"Since when has Alethdariel become your homeland?" Aranok scoffed.

"Since I was born and brought up there, dummy."

Aranok stifled a chuckle at being able to bait Ariana yet again.

"Oh, I forgot about that."

Ariana thumped him in the arm.

"Ahem." Harnez cleared his throat.

Grald jumped. "Whoops, sorry, Lord Harnez. I haven't rested properly since we arrived in the city."

"My apologies, Lord Harnez," Ariana said. "My half-brother isn't exactly used to being around humans other than my mother or me. We don't get out of Alethdar much."

"That explains your lack of knowledge then. Alethdariel prefers to ignore the existence of the Dungeons. The only one which was built there, was cleansed and turned into a storage facility of some kind, I believe."

"Are you referring to the Mage Library?" Ariana sent an incredulous glance at Aranok. I never knew it was an abandoned dungeon. Although that does explain a couple of things about the place. Hmmm, Aranok doesn't seem surprised. Maybe it's something that Elven Bloods are taught?

"It would be an ideal place to house such dangerous knowledge, so yes, that is probably the one." Harnez turned back to the map and sighed. "I conferred with King Groilin, and we agreed this one is far too close to the city for comfort."

"Why are you bothering to send a party in at all?" Aranok asked. "Surely if there are creatures in there at all, the safest thing to do would be to leave it alone."

"There are several reasons that we need to clear it out. Firstly, the land there is fertile and has been unused for centuries. With the troubles the king is experiencing in the Southern Spires with the supposed Franieren Bandits, he requires extra supplies and wants to site a new village there. Secondly ..." his voice trailed off and he looked into the distance.

"Did you lose someone there?" Ariana's gentle voice jolted him out of his reverie.

"Yes. My younger sister. We were acting upon a dare from one of our friends by exploring the ruins and she just... disappeared." He shook himself and coughed. "I would like whoever goes to try and find some trace of her. I do not believe, unlike my family, that she fell down some hole and died from her injuries."

Ariana exchanged a glance with her brother. "I see."

Harnez regained his composure "According to the village closest to the castle, there have been many such disappearances, as well as stories of vampires, werewolves and other such monsters that roam the countryside."

"And you consider stories a danger?" Aranok's scepticism seemed to irritate the lord.

"I conferred with King Groilin, and we agreed it is far too close to Valdez for comfort. If the creatures within are real, we need to remove such an infestation immediately."

"And the supposed wealth of gemstones and gold below the castle helps of course," the half elf muttered. Harnez ignored him.

Grald glowered at the map. "Why didn't the King send his troops in?" he asked.

"They are currently tied up in a border skirmish with Franier over the pass through the Spires, as well as their bandit hunting and general patrol duties in the kingdom." Harnez looked annoyed at the notion that his king wouldn't help and pointed at the flag that indicated Castle Grof. "I paid for a large party of local mercenaries and adventurers to infiltrate the Dungeon. They got through the underground tunnels as far as a Graveyard before they were attacked by Vampires. Shilir was the only one to get out of the Dungeon alive."

"What about afterward? I mean, you had Shilir's account to back you up," Aranok asked. "Surely the King would have helped you then."

"I attempted to persuade the King to lend me half a brigade to cleanse the Dungeon, but he refused to even consider the suggestion." Harnez shrugged, his weariness with the situation filling his voice.

Aranok rolled his eyes at Ariana.

"So, you sent Shilir to get Grald and put together another party to go into the Dungeon."

"Yes. Warrior Grald is famed as a fighter and Shilir felt that he would be the ideal choice to lead..."

"Oh, no." Grald backed up waving his hands "I don't lead anywhere. I thought Shilir would be leading, it's the only reason I agreed to come along."

The Valdierian lord raised an eyebrow at the barbarian.

"Even I have heard the tales of the Royal Crypt at Coptir and the incursion into Giranath."

Grald snorted derisively.

"You believe what the bards tell of me? I've only just bought my freedom from the Lord of Southnra. Those 'exploits' the bards tell of were undertaken at his behest and I barely managed to escape Giranath. I lost ten men on that trip, and I am not being held responsible for the wellbeing of this one."

"Oh. I didn't realise that. Obviously Shilir didn't do his research well enough." Harnez looked inquiringly at Aranok who backed away with his hands up.

"Ariana and I have not yet made any decision on whether or not we are even going to help you." He looked at his sister, who sighed.

"I think we need a little more detail and to sleep on it before we can make a decision. Especially as Grald is reluctant to take the lead in such a patently dangerous mission." She looked at the Lord. "And I should consult with the Guild of Magic Users."

"Very well. As Shilir is the only survivor of the last party, I am sending him to Galivor, Reldheim, Alethdariel and Franier to endeavour to persuade them to put aside their differences and attack the Dungeons." The Lord moved back to his desk and sat down. "I believe there is something stirring up the creatures and should it be necessary, a concerted effort would be needed to deal with all of the dungeons at once."

"Sounds like a good idea." Aranok approved and looked at Grald. "Where do you stand then?"

"I'm happy to go on the quest; I just don't want to lead it," he replied, looking a little shamefaced.

"I can understand that." Aranok turned back to Harnez. "You'd be expecting me to lead this party then? How many more people would you be adding to it?"

"As many as I could. I'd hope that the pair of you would…"

"We'll think about what you are proposing," Ariana interrupted, turning for the door.

"Where are you going?" the Lord frowned at her.

"I am Alethdariel's Guild of Magic Users Liaison. I spent most of the day reporting to the Valdierien Guild on an urgent matter." Ariana stretched "I need to sleep and talk to Aranok about this little adventure, especially as it sounds so dangerous."

"Where are you staying?" Harnez asked.

"We were going to stay at the Mountain's Shadow, but Grald's little fight put paid to that, we're likely to get arrested again if we go back there."

Grald hung his head and groaned. "The dwarf started it."

"Why don't you stay across the way at the Royal Tower Inn?" Harnez suggested.

"We can't afford to stay there. It's the most expensive inn in the city; only nobles stay there." Ariana's eyes almost popped out of their sockets.

"Technically we are nobles, remember?" Aranok stifled a laugh.

"It's still too expensive." She shook her head stubbornly.

"I'll send a message across that you are staying as my guests," Lord Harnez told Ariana in a soothing voice. "That way you don't have to chance the streets in a search for somewhere to stay, and I'll have an opportunity to locate at least another two party members. I will also deal with the City Watch; it would not do for you to be arrested before you can make your decision."

Aranok bowed. "Thank you, milord. That would be most welcome."

Harnez smiled, pulling a piece of notepaper out of a drawer. As he wrote, he spoke "I shall pay for anything you require and in the morning we can talk again." He rang a bell and Shilir reappeared. "Shilir, take them across to the Royal Tower and give Mistress Dinra this note."

Shilir bowed "Yes Lord Harnez."

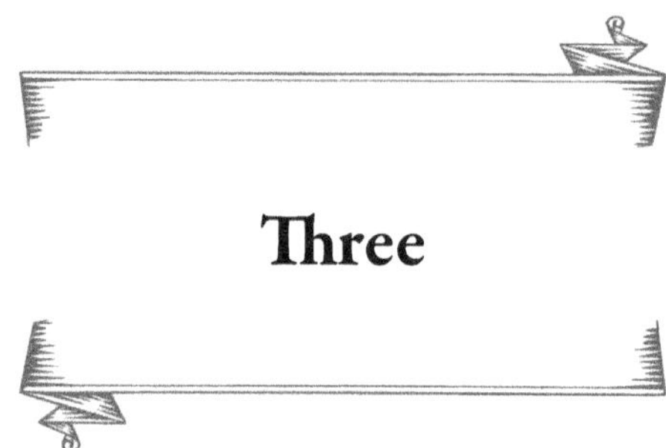

Three

Mistress Dinra ushered them into the suite she had decided was worthy of the guests of Lord Harnez.

"He's done a lot for me over the years, has Lord Harnez. I'll be happy to accommodate anything you need."

"Is there someone who can take a message for me?" Ariana dropped her bags on the floor beside a comfortable looking cushioned chair and sighed as she sat down.

"My youngest son is the Inn Runner. I'll send him up to you." Mistress Dinra curtseyed, backed out of the door and shut it quietly behind her.

Grald looked around, opened a bedroom door and gave a low whistle.

"By Tyr's Great Golden Genitalia, this is a costly place."

"Oh?" Aranok put his stuff beside Ariana, who was busy on a nearby table with parchment, ink and wax, and wandered over to peer through the door. "Very nice. You taking that one?"

"May as well. I like red velvet; doesn't show the blood." The barbarian laughed at his own joke as he disappeared into the bedroom.

Aranok opened the door next to the room Grald has chosen.

"Hmm, blue. I'm not sure it's my colour, but I'll make do." He retrieved his bags and ambled inside.

Ariana finished her message and sealed it with a spell just as there was a knock at the door.

"Come in."

A young lad wearing a dark blue sash with the Inn's symbol on it and a matching floppy velvet cap opened the door. He bowed.

"Mama sent me to take your message for you. The charge for my services shall be added to your bill."

Ariana smiled. "Thank you. Return to me when you are done, and I shall give you a silver for your trouble." She passed the message to him, and he slid it into the pouch attached to his sash, bowed and left the room, shutting the door as quietly as his mother had.

Aranok poked his head out of the room he had chosen.

"Haven't you got settled in yet, Ariana?"

She stood up, collected her bag and went to the third of the rooms off the sitting room.

"Just about to get sorted. I'm tired, so I'll meet you and Grald downstairs in the common room later."

Aranok watched the door shut behind his sister with a certain amount of concern on his face.

The sound of the door shutting seemed to trigger Grald emerging from his room.

"What's going on?" he asked.

"Brother-sister stuff don't worry about it. So, tell me about this dungeon thing. I know what Harnez wants out of it, but what do you want?" Aranok shut the door to his room behind him.

Grald came out and smiled.

"Fancy a pint? We can talk about it downstairs."

"That'd be a good idea; you already owe me a drink from earlier." Aranok grinned and the two of them left the suite.

An hour or so later, the two men were already on their third tankard of mead. Ariana came down to find them swapping scar stories and entertaining the common room's other inhabitants by stripping off various pieces of clothing to display the scar they were talking about.

Mistress Dinra hurried over to Ariana.

"I'm glad you're here, Lady. Could you ask your companions to calm down? We normally get a lot of the local residents in here, but I've already seen three of my regulars come in and leave again."

Ariana sighed.

"This happens all the time around Aranok. I'll sort them out, Mistress Dinra. Can you bring us whatever meal is currently on offer from the kitchen, please? The food should help things a little."

The Innkeeper smiled with relief.

"Thank you. Is there anything special that you would like for yourself?"

"If you have any Chocacao from the Southern Islands, I would appreciate some." Ariana thanked her with a small bow and headed toward the table where her brother was currently showing off the long scar on his back.

"I did that when I was a toddler," she said loudly, sitting down across from him. "He left a broadhead arrow head in the main room, where I could reach and I grabbed it. He didn't notice I was in the room, and I whacked him with the arrow in a fit of rage that I was being ignored. Mother had Father sit on him while she stitched it back up."

Aranok glared at her as he dropped his tunic back down.

"You promised to never talk about that."

"I had to say something to stop us getting thrown out of another inn. Mistress Dinra asked me to stop you two driving her regulars away." Ariana frowned as she took in the state of her brother. "And you two haven't eaten either have you?"

They looked away from her and Ariana bit her lip to stop herself laughing as her older brother took on a guilty expression. A moment later, they both shook their heads silently.

"Just as well that I ordered us some food, isn't it." Then she couldn't hold it any longer and burst out laughing. The food arrived and put an end to her giggle fit.

Grald and Aranok dived on the roast goose, potatoes and bread as if they hadn't eaten in a week. Ariana stayed quiet on the subject of table manners, despite the irritated looks Mistress Dinra sent her way, until she judged that they'd had enough food to soak up the mead,

"So, what are we going to do, Aranok?" Ariana asked, soaking a slice of bread in her gravy. "We have to make a decision at some point."

"I'm not sure about this Ariana. I have to get back to Alethdariel." Aranok picked at his bread, flicking crumbs across the table at her.

"You mean you have to get back to Liana." His sister raised an eyebrow.

"I told her I would bring her a promise ring from the Viraldian Elves."

"We picked that up on the way here. What's the problem then?"

"I have to take it back to her."

"And you will!" Ariana rolled her eyes "Aranok, Grald can't cleanse the Dungeon by himself."

"Harnez can find a couple of other mugs to go with him." Aranok glanced at the barbarian. "No offence."

"None taken. I'm even having second thoughts about it now." Grald belched and winced as Ariana frowned at him. "Sorry."

Before she could say anything further, a boy wearing a green tabard embroidered with a crossed pair of gold wands entered the common room and strode straight over to Ariana.

He bowed. "Lady Ariana of Alethdariel. You are summoned to a Moot at the Guild."

"The Guild?" Grald asked Aranok.

"The Guild of Magic Users." The ranger stretched. "That's one of Archmage Reldalliam's personal runners. Weren't you paying attention to anything my sister said earlier?"

Grald shrugged and concentrated on his food. "Not really."

Grabbing her cloak from the back of her chair and swinging it around her shoulders, Ariana sighed, "Lead on, Youngling." To her brother, she said, "Aranok, I'll be back as soon as I can. Try not to get into any trouble."

"Since when do I get into trouble?" Aranok protested.

Ariana contented herself with shaking her head and followed the page out of the Inn.

"She seemed to be expecting him." Grald poured Aranok another mug of mead.

"She sent a message out earlier. I wouldn't be surprised if that was her answer." Aranok stuffed another piece of bread in his mouth and washed it down with a long draught from his mug.

"Who is Liana?" Grald asked.

"She's the daughter of Queen Aletaraenia of Alethdariel."

"Is she a Princess?"

"Of course she is." Aranok blinked and sighed. "She's beautiful. Long hair the colour of copperleaf leaves in the autumn, eyes as blue as sapphires..." Aranok trailed off into a reflective silence.

"Sounds like your friend is in love," a melodic voice interrupted.

"It does sound that way," Grald said as he turned to look at the newcomer. He blinked.

"WELL, THIS IS AN INTERESTING occurrence, Sire." The Jar remarked from its pedestal beside the throne. "I thought she'd vanished when Galindren was lost to the Humans, is she still our... yours?"

The Aracan Katuvana clapped its hands together twice. A tiny Gremlin appeared out of nowhere and bowed deeply.

"Bring the miniatures," the Jar commanded.

The Gremlin bowed again, spun on the spot and disappeared. Moments later, it was back with a large, gilded Ironwood box, which it presented to the figure. As the Aracan Katuvana opened the box, another pair of Gremlins set up a table in front of the throne.

The Aracan Katuvana laid the miniatures out on the table. There were thirteen spaces in the velvet-lined box, but only twelve diminutive figures. The Aracan Katuvana examined each one carefully then selected one.

Rising, he strode over to the window where the scene through the barbarian's eyes was playing out. The ancient goblin picked the Jar up and followed him.

The Aracan Katuvana placed the miniature onto a red plinth in front of the window and made a small gesture over it. The miniature blinked.

"This is most definitely the one, Lord. Thank the Darkness that she has stayed true."

The Aracan Katuvana considered the miniature and the barbarian whose picture had appeared in the top left of the window.

"Would you like to activate this agent, Sire?" the Jar sounded uneasy, as if it were unable to gauge the Aracan's mood. "She could cause much chaos in Valdez at your command."

The Aracan Katuvana shook his head, his hood flaring with the movement. It allowed some of the candlelight to fall upon his eyes, glinting blood red in the shadows.

Snapping his fingers over the miniature made a picture of the agent's face appear in the top right of the window. With another gesture, the Aracan Katuvana created a frame around the picture of the barbarian, and with a final snap of the fingers, the frame glowed pink.

The Jar spoke to the barbarian.

"I am in love with this person. I will allow her to do anything she wishes."

The pink glow deepened as the spell took hold.

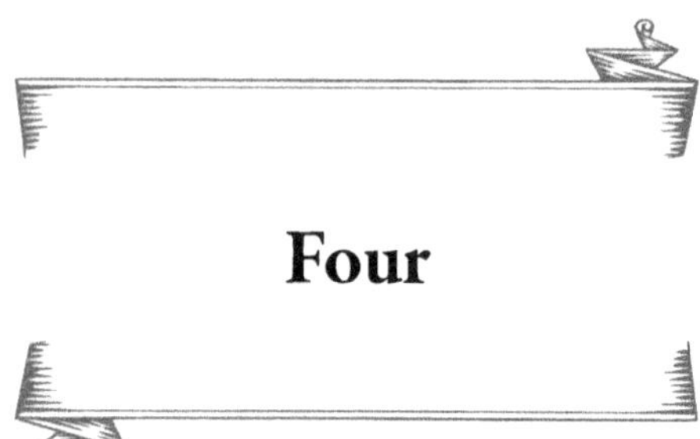

Four

Grald stared at the newcomer with deep admiration. She was tall with a shapely figure that seemed more exotic than even the most beautiful of the Southern Islanders he'd ever seen. Her Ebony skin contrasted sharply with her long silver hair, long strands hanging loose around a perfectly chiselled face. A pair of large pale gold eyes seemed to draw him in and before he knew what was happening, he felt a hot flush centring on his loins. "Well, hello..." he breathed.

She smiled. "Hello yourself, Barbarian. I hear you have a little party going on."

"It's none of your business." Aranok pushed himself upright, glaring at the newcomer.

"We're going to raid a Dungeon of Doom," Grald replied, feeling more than a little breathless and wondering why his heart was beating so fast.

"That sounds interesting. May I join you?"

"Be my guest." Grald gestured to the stool beside him, "Can I get you a drink?"

The newcomer nodded.

"A mug of mead would be pleasant."

Grald all but jumped up and ran over to the bar.

Aranok looked at the newcomer.

"What are you doing here?"

"I was in the neighbourhood, and I thought I would drop by."

"Erendell, I have known you for a little over a hundred years. You never just drop by."

"Aww, Aranok, we played together as children before little Ariana was born. Can't you just be pleased that an old friend wants to see you?"

"No. Last time you dropped by, Ariana and I ended up on the plains of Reldheim fighting Urakhs We only just got out of there alive! Where were you?" Aranok paused for a long moment, tapping his finger against his lips and looking up into the air between them. "Oh yes, I remember, carousing with the dwarves in Laikholm."

"Okay, so I've got you into a little bit of trouble over the years…"

At that point, Grald came back. He placed a mug in front of Erendell and sat back down, slowly becoming aware of the chill to the air.

"What's the matter?"

"Aranok and I are just renewing our friendship," Erendell told him, as she sipped from her mug.

Grald felt his chest tighten.

"You know, Aranok?" His voice seemed harsh even to him.

"He and I grew up together. We're old friends."

Grald glared at Aranok, suddenly feeling jealous.

"Old friends, eh?" Aranok held his hand up.

"Liana, Erendell and I were in the same nursery group when we were children, Grald."

"Erendell is a pretty name." Grald ignored Aranok's explanation, but it loosened the knot inside him.

"It's short for Erendelliana. It means Dark Flower in Viraldian Elvish. My Mother is Viraldian, and I've inherited her colouring." She flashed a raised eyebrow at him, daring him to say anything.

"I think your name suits you," Grald sighed, gazing at Erendell, his eyelids drooping and a soft smile spreading across his face. "I've never worried about colour or race when admiring a

"Thank you." The dark elf shot a look of consternation at Aranok, who shrugged and said:

"I've only just met him, but it looks like you have an admirer, Erendell."

She rolled her eyes at him and smiled at Grald who leaned towards her and smiled back.

Aranok stifled a laugh and finished his mead, then waved his mug at the barmaid.

"Bring another round over please, m'dear."

The barmaid beamed at him.

Ariana returned an hour later with a dwarf wearing hardened leather armour and carrying a mace.

"Hello Erendell, it's been a while," she said as she removed her cloak. "The Archmage told me you'd been seen in the city."

"It has been a long while since I saw you last, Ariana." Erendell shrugged. "I've been here and there doing all sorts of things; some of it even legal. Has Aranok managed to capture Liana's attention yet?"

Ariana laughed at the expression on her brother's face

"Not entirely. What brings you here?" She waved one hand around the common room.

"I happened to be in Valdez and spotted the two of you coming this way earlier. It took me a while to find you, but I was curious and wanted to see what my oldest friends were up to." The elf smiled at her friend.

Aranok snorted. "You mean you were stalking us."

"I did follow you for a little while, and it was just as well; that fish barrow wouldn't have exploded by itself, and I'm rather hurt that you didn't recognise my fireball." The dark elf pouted.

"I recognised your voice, but we were a little too preoccupied with getting away to look for you," Ariana replied wryly.

"That would do it." Erendell laughed and Grald joined in.

Ariana blinked and stared at the barbarian, then looked across at her brother, who shook his head.

"So, what did the Guild say and why have you got an underdweller following you around?" Aranok asked.

The dwarf raised one eyebrow at the epithet but stayed silent and still behind Ariana.

"We've been asked to cleanse the Dungeon of Doom, Erendell." Ariana turned to the dwarf. "Arnhammen, this is Aranok, my brother; Grald, a recently freed barbarian warrior; and Erendell, an old friend. This is Arnhammen Towerston. The Guild assigned him to be my Mage Protector."

The Dwarf bowed to those assembled around the table.

"Am I not enough of a Mage Protector for the Guild then?" Aranok asked.

"It's not that, brother, I have been ordered to take part in Lord Harnez's Dungeon Cleansing and the Guild feels you should be able to follow your own path." Ariana laid one hand on his arm, trying to make him feel better.

"As if I'd leave my younger sister with two strangers." Aranok took her hand in his and kissed the back of it. "Where you go, I go. Mother would never forgive me otherwise."

"Is yon Drow no part o't'Party then?" Arnhammen asked, pulling a stool over from another table and sitting down.

"I'm interested in helping out if you want me, Ariana." Erendell waved her mug amicably. "I haven't got anything to do at the moment and I love a bit of adventure. What about you, Grald?"

"I'm definitely up for it now." The barbarian linked eyes with the dark elf and after a moment, she looked away, the colour of her cheeks darkening.

"Well, that seals it," Aranok snorted. "If you think I'm going to let two strangers and a troublesome dark elf escort my sister into a Dungeon that has already claimed the lives of one party..."

Ariana beamed at her brother, relieved that she hadn't needed to argue him round.

"We're to go back to Lord Harnez in the morning to collect our supplies. He's going to provide everything."

"Is this it then? You, me, Grald, Erendell and a dwarf." He frowned. "Can't we take a city guard or two with us?"

"I be worth three o'them," Arnhammen growled.

"Where did you train?" Grald asked.

"As a Dwarfling, I trained with the Laikholm division of the Reldheimian Army." Arnhammen nodded his thanks to the barmaid who set a mug of foamy ale in front of him. "Ah, thank ye darlin'." He took a deep draught of ale before continuing. "I took part in the raids on the north end of Lakurakh when I came of age and was seconded to Laikholm's Guild of Magic Users as a Mage Protector fifty years ago."

Grald nodded.

"That's a good run. You have any problems with where we're going?"

"I go where my assigned Mage goes. I fear nothing with my mace in my hand." Arnhammen finished his ale and stretched.

"I'd better get some sleep then. The last time I led a party like this I spent far too much time awake waiting for a Lych to jump out on me..." Aranok ambled off to his room.

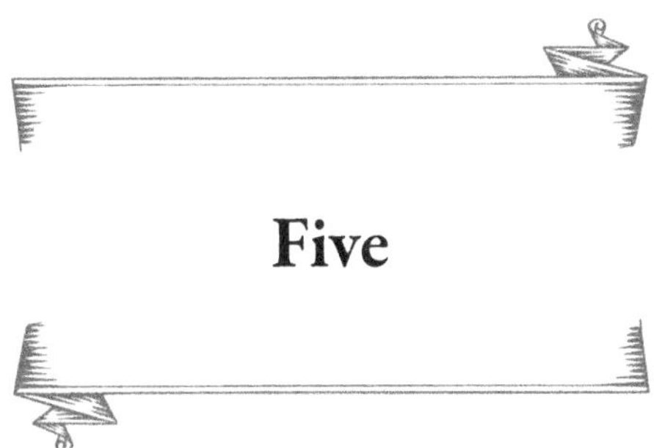

Five

The journey out to Castle Grof the next morning was uneventful. Grald spent most of the time alternating between trying to impress Erendell and just staring at her, sighing every so often.

Halfway through the ride, Ariana abandoned her brother's side and the tactical discussion going on between Arnhammen and Aranok. She pushed her mare to catch up with Erendell where she was dazzling Grald with her wit.

"Would you mind lending my brother the benefit of your experience, Grald?" she said with a bright smile.

"Not at all, Lady." Grald bowed in his saddle and reined his horse back. "This stretch of the road seems very quiet but keep an eye open."

"We will," Erendell assured him.

The two women rode silently for a while.

Around them, the wind rustled the tall grass that covered this part of Valdier, disturbing the crickets' song. A small blue, rabbit like creature hopped into the road in front of them, its nose to the ground as it followed a scent across their path into the grass on the opposite side of the road. There was a growl, a rustle and a squeal; the blue animal appeared at the side of the road as they rode past, a small mouse in its jaws, blood dribbling down and staining the creature's fur purple.

"Nice to see that the hunting out here is as plentiful as ever," Erendell remarked flipping a respectful salute at the animal. "Harabbin are almost extinct in Franier. I could make a killing in the fur market at Fron with only a few Harabbin pelts."

The Harabbin ignored them and hopped away into the tall grass, carrying its meal.

"There don't seem to be many people out here," Ariana shrugged. "Maybe the local hunters are busy."

"This border war would use up men at a frightening rate," Erendell said. "I'm surprised that the King even has enough men to staff the city watch."

There was a burst of laughter from behind them.

"It seems that the men are getting on well back there." Ariana glanced back at the three warriors.

"I thought Aranok was going to end up a red smear on the floor when he called Arnhammen 'Underdweller.'" Erendell shook her head. "You'd think that the son of a prominent Alethdariellian lord would know better."

Ariana sighed. "Nokkie isn't exactly known for his tact or diplomacy though. Why do you think the queen agreed to let him be my Mage Protector for this trip?"

"He didn't upset someone did he?" Erendell laid her reins on her mare's neck and stretched.

"The Prince Consort; Aranok told him that he was a pompous windbag and didn't deserve Liana as a stepdaughter." Ariana laughed at Erendell's expression.

"I'm surprised that the queen is still allowing him to court Liana after that," the dark elf muttered.

"She just laughed and suggested that he get out of the city for a while," Ariana giggled. "Then Liana asked him to bring her a Viraldian promise ring back for their betrothal ceremony and I was practically dragged out of Alethdar by the scruff of my neck."

"There's nothing like love to motivate a man." Erendell exchanged a look with Ariana; they both looked back at Aranok and started laughing louder.

He frowned and pushed his horse into a trot to catch up with them.

"What on earth are you two laughing about?" he asked as he rode up beside him. "Nothing much," the women said together.

"Hmm. Well, the castle is just up ahead." He pointed to the right of the road where silver birch and copperleaf trees rose from the top of a small hill.

"Are we stopping to eat and check what we're doing before we go in?" Erendell yawned. "I need to have a nap."

"Fine, as long as you don't eat any Copperleaf and berry bread," Aranok told her as they left the road and headed for the trees.

"Why is that important?" Grald asked.

"It's not really, but I hate the smell of the stuff," Aranok replied.

Erendell rolled her eyes. "He's the only elf I know who doesn't like it."

"Considering how loopy it makes you elves, I'm glad he doesn't," Ariana retorted.

Erendell shrugged. "Not my fault."

"Never mind that. Let's get on with what we're here for." Aranok dismounted under a silver birch. "We'll go further in on foot."

"Harnez was right when he said that the Guardian Castles were left in ruins." Grald surveyed the area around the entrance to the Dungeon. Large blocks of stone lay where they had tumbled from the curtain wall and the majority of the inside walls were nothing more than humps in the sod, the occasional crumbled brick showing through the grass.

"I thought the entrances were all bricked up?" Ariana frowned at the neatly presented Ironwood door with the carved steel inlaid Tower and Eye symbol on both doors.

"Shilir said it was clear when he and his party got here. Maybe Lord Harnez had it done." Grald shrugged.

"It seems t'me that there be too much coincidence in this little adventure," Arnhammen muttered.

Erendell sank down onto the grass.

"I'll take a quick nap. Wake me when you are ready to go or I'll wake myself in half an hour, whichever comes first." She wrapped herself into her cloak and was asleep before Aranok had time to object.

Ariana shook her head. "She never changes."

Aranok decided to ignore them. He sat down on the grass opposite the door and checked the map Shilir had given them one more time.

There wasn't much detail on it, just a rundown of the traps his party had encountered along the corridors that they had scouted out. Shilir had used an All-Seeing Eye spell to find out the rest of the layout.

Aranok remembered Harnez's eyes as he briefed them that morning. Shilir had been off with Ariana and Arnhammen, something about spells and magical items.

Grald had volunteered Erendell and himself to sort out the supplies and packhorses. Aranok found himself alone in the study with Lord Harnez.

"Remember Sir Aranok, you must retrieve the Heart Crystal and get it out into the sunlight, or the Dungeon will regenerate."

"I understand, Lord Harnez," Aranok replied.

"I must have that Heart Crystal!" Harnez had been resolute, thumping his fist down on the table. Aranok bowed.

"You may take anything else that you want from the Dungeon. Bring the Heart Crystal out and back to me. That is by far the most important thing."

"Very well, milord."

Aranok had wondered at the time if something else was going on, but before he could ask, the others had returned.

"I'll wager you a silver piece that he's thinking about Liana," Erendell murmured sleepily to Ariana as she woke up.

"Nah, he's wondering how on earth to get himself out of trouble this time," Ariana replied from where she sat checking her potions.

The sound of his sister and Erendell laughing brought Aranok out of his reverie.

"Neither actually," he said, laying the map out on a nearby block of stone. "I was wondering how I ended up with a sister with no safety sense. Ward us please, Ariana."

The young mage grimaced and concentrated for a few seconds, sending balls of red light out to rest in a rough circle around them.

"I believe it would be a good idea to plan where we are going before we enter the dungeon, rather than just blundering around." Aranok beckoned to the rest of the group. They gathered around the map. "Shilir did a good job of detailing what rooms and corridors there are. His party went straight up past the crossroads and through this middle door. That's where they ran into trouble. The guard post is manned by Vampires on the other side."

"Then t'intelligence would suggest we take a different route," Arnhammen surmised.

"Yes. I thought we'd go through this door at the end of the right hand passage and continue up this corridor here, until we reach the door at the top of the Dungeon." Aranok traced his proposed route out with his finger.

"What about this route; through the left hand door, up this corridor and through this entrance here," Erendell said, pointing.

"Into this little complex of rooms?" Grald sounded dubious as he examined the map. "Shilir thought there was something very strong living in those rooms. He showed me this map when he picked me up in Jinra. He didn't catch more than a glimpse of it, but he said it gave off an incredibly evil aura."

"Why do we need to use these corridors at all?" Ariana asked her voice muffled as she rifled through her bag of Holding. "Ah ha!" She pulled out a large copper plated cube.

"What in Tyr's name be ye doing with a Digger Mech, Lady?" Arnhammen said his eyes wide as he watched her. "I ha'nae seen one o'them since I were a wee Dwarfling at home in Reldheim."

"I picked it up in Laikholm when Aranok, Erendell and I were helping with the Urakh Troubles."

"What are you suggesting Ariana?" Aranok asked.

"We could take your proposed route, but instead of going through this top door which would take us straight into the Treasury, where there are likely to be a lot of creatures, why don't we stop here," she placed her finger on the east corridor roughly half way up, "and dig our own tunnel into the centre of the Dungeon?"

"That sounds like the best plan that I've heard yet." Grald cracked his knuckles and stretched as Ariana put the Mech away. "What do you think Aranok?"

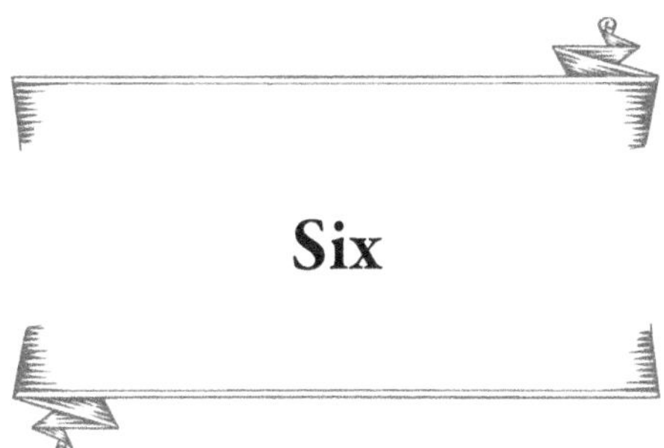

Six

"That would indeed be an excellent Plan, if it were not for the fact that you are watching, Master. What would you like to do, Milord?" The Jar grinned.

The Aracan Katuvana pondered for a moment, his head on his hand. Then he used both hands in a book opening gesture. One of the books from a pile on the table beside the throne floated into his lap and opened.

"Ah, the Grof Dungeon profile," the Jar murmured.

The Aracan flicked through the pages to a map of the Dungeon and spent a few moments tracing his finger around the rooms. He laid the book aside, still open and went over to the window. A brief hand gesture later and the face of the Grof Custodian appeared.

She was a shapely elf with long deep red-brown hair, blue eyes and skin so pale it resembled a fine, translucent linen cloth.

"Dearest Lord and Master, how may I serve you?" Her voice chimed musically as she curtsied deeply. It was deep enough to show her ample cleavage in the low neck of a deep red dress and the Aracan Katuvana was clearly mesmerised by the sight.

"You will be having a party of adventurers arrive in your Dungeon shortly, Lych Mistress," the Jar told her.

Katuvana recovered his senses and waved his hand over the bottom left corner of the window and a map of the Dungeon appeared. He pointed to the spot where the Party's planned tunnel would start. He traced a line across to the Heart Crystal Dais.

The Lych Mistress made a pretty moue of irritation.

"Again? I only just rid myself of the last group." She appeared to study something in front of her. "A tunnel? Hmmm, I have some Hellhounds available, Lord. I could build a guard post between the Library and the Lair. Hellhounds are perfect guard dogs."

Katuvana nodded.

"Excellent idea, Lych Mistress. Oversee the work personally," the Jar said as the elf curtsied again and the view returned to that of the party.

"That Lych Mistress is one fine figure of an Elf – mayhap you could make her your Mistress?" the Jar suggested slyly.

The Aracan Katuvana growled, and the Jar seemed almost to jump.

"Of course, not Master, I would never suggest..."

The Aracan Katuvana shook his head and sat back on the throne, facing the window.

THE GROUP MOVED INTO the Dungeon, leaving their horses hobbled in a clearing near the entrance.

Erendell produced a Trap Hunter and set it to automatic. Within three hundred yards of the entrance, the globe detected several different traps. Erendell disarmed them with barely a bead of sweat decorating her brow.

"Those weren't on the map," Aranok frowned as they moved past the disarmed area.

"It was almost a year ago since Shilir came down here," Grald shrugged. "They've obviously fortified their weak spots."

Aranok started swearing as they found another three traps in the crossroad.

"Erendell, deal with them."

"I can't disarm these, they're Aethyric traps," Erendell snapped. "I left home before my mother started teaching that particular lesson."

"I thought she kicked you out," he said, glaring at the dark elf. Erendell's face darkened.

"I can deal with them," Ariana soothed her brother. She knelt beside each one and disarmed it carefully.

"Thank you, Ariana." Erendell smiled at the young mage. "Aranok is getting rather tense."

"That's okay. He's not at his best underground."

"What Elf truly is?" Erendell laughed. "Even my mother's people live high up in the Under City where it's airier."

Following the corridor to the right, they encountered nothing. The walls ran with glowing green ooze that lit the passageway. It puddled in cracks and overflowed to create tiny waterfalls, before disappearing through the floor with a gurgling, sucking noise.

"That's disgusting." Ariana wrinkled her nose.

"It does sound a wee bit strange, Lady Mage," Arnhammen agreed with her.

On the ceiling, white moths with black skull-like patterns congregated and chose to flutter around the party.

"Don't let the moths touch your skin," Erendell cautioned them. "They're poisonous."

"How d'ye know Drow? Ye never lived below ground, I wager." Arnhammen sniffed and grimaced.

"No, but my mother did. I'm only half Drow by blood," Erendell said. "She taught me about much more than just magic."

At the end of the corridor Ariana fashioned a small bird golem out of glowing ooze and sent it under the door to scout ahead, shutting her eyes to better concentrate. The rest of the party took the moment to relax and have a drink.

"Was ye maether a mage?" Arnhammen asked Erendell, passing her a small flask.

"Eliethorendraelliana is her full name," Aranok told him. "She is one of the greatest mages that ever existed, but her story is a tragic one."

"My mother has suffered much because of her power. It is her duty to teach those who come to the Mage Library in Alethdariel, as she is the only one strong enough to help them." Erendell blinked rapidly, moisture shining in her eyes.

"She's a marvellous teacher," Ariana said softly, opening her eyes.

"What did you see?" Aranok asked.

"Steady on, Aranok, the Lady has only just returned!" Arnhammen held out one hand. "Gie her a minute to come to herself."

"It's all right, Arnhammen." Ariana smiled at the dwarf. "The corridor ahead is patrolled by Skeletons. They move in groups of five and should be easy enough to deal with – if Arnhammen is up to it."

"I hae ne'er been more ready, Lady." The dwarf looked eager to go.

"Then let us away to battle the Undead in our bid to free this world of evil!" Erendell proclaimed as if reciting some ancient battle cry.

Grald and Arnhammen looked at Erendell as if she'd grown horns. Aranok gagged and turned away, unable to speak, and Ariana grinned.

"It's ok," she said. "She's eating Copperleaf and Berry Bread." She pointed at the wedge of bread in the dark elf's hand.

"Huh?" Grald sounded confused.

"Don't worry about it," Aranok said, swilling his mouth out with water. "Erendell put that stuff away."

"Oh, all right." Erendell folded a napkin around the wedge and put it into her knapsack.

Erendell disarmed the alarm and gas traps that she found by the door and unlocked it with a twist of a pick. They moved cautiously through and into the next corridor.

Here there was no glowing ooze, so Ariana produced a Mage Globe and whispered to it. It glowed a soft yellow that made Erendell's golden eyes gleam in the borrowed light.

"She's so beautiful," Grald whispered longingly to Aranok as they made their way up the passage.

"Be careful, Grald. Erendell is nearly one hundred and eight years old and has had at least four human lovers that I know of. She'll break your heart." Aranok shook his head when the barbarian's face turned stubborn. To change the subject he asked, "Do you have any family?"

"Yes. I have a younger sister, Freya."

"Where is she at the moment?"

"She's a Pleasure House Slave in Jira. I used to be a Gladiator Slave there as well. A merchant who won a lot of money betting on me bought me and set me free. Now all I have to do is buy her free."

"Is that why you're adventuring? You never did tell me when we were talking last night." Aranok looked around the corridor they were walking up. "It's too quiet."

Grald wasn't really paying much attention to Aranok.

"Yes, Lord Harnez promised me enough gold to pay off at least half of her price. I'm hoping to pick up some more here and I have a third of her price already stashed away."

They reached the point that Ariana suggested they dig from without encountering any Skeletons.

"That was strange. I expected at least one skirmish on the way up here," the mage remarked as she pulled the Digger Mech out of her bag. The copper cube sat on the ground quiescent as she attached a leather cord to her wrist and another to a loop at the back of the cube.

"Aye Lady t'is strangely quiet, but I shall nae count on it staying that way." Arnhammen set out four blue quartz cubes two on either side of the party, setting them down in the centre and began to pray over his medallion of Tyr.

The cubes glowed, rose from the ground and began to spin around them, just over their heads. A translucent barrier surrounded them with a pale blue light.

"Why in the Mother's name have you put a leash on that thing, Ariana?" Erendell frowned, examining the cube minutely, her curiosity getting the better of her.

"It's just in case I forget that I've set it off." Ariana fiddled with the Mech, opening a flap, turning a dial and pressing a button or two, seemingly randomly. "They just dig continuously, and should we be interrupted, and I don't get a chance to stop it, I'd lose it."

"Aye, Mechs o'any sort are on the expensive side o'costly. We would nae want tae lose it." The dwarf grunted through his prayer. With a final smattering of Dwarfish, he finished and kissed the medallion. "There, that should do it."

"I hope I'm not prying, Arnhammen, but what exactly does this barrier do? It doesn't look very substantial," Aranok asked.

"'Tis a Warding o' Holy Tyr. Should any undead chance upon it, they will feel Lord Tyr's wrath upon their unholy forms," The dwarf said.

Aranok didn't feel confident about the almost non-existent shield, so he put Grald and Erendell on opposite sides of the blue lit area and set himself just beside Ariana as the Mech began its work.

The small copper cube unfolded and expanded itself into what looked like a metal gremlin with clawed scoops instead of paws. The Mech leapt into the air to cling to the wall near the ceiling with its feet, then rapidly dug with its front paws, sending rock flying until it broke through the stone facing on the wall. Once through that, the Mech began to dig down until its feet were on the floor. As soon as the Mech had created a shallow niche it expanded again, becoming taller than Grald and wider than Arnhammen.

"Ye set it to the barbarian's height? My compliments, Lady, ye hae been studying the rudiments o'tunnelling it seems." Arnhammen said.

Ariana blushed. "It seemed like a good idea when I bought it. The Mech usually needs a second Mech behind it, shoring up the walls and ceiling, but Eliethor added a spell to its body that solidifies the dirt it leaves behind. She said it should stop any cave ins but could still be dug through by other creatures."

"Mother always was oddly practical for someone who lived with her head in the clouds." Erendell sniffed.

The Mech moved forward and began to dig, shifting the loose soil behind it. As the soil left the thing's scoops, it shrank to the size of peas.

"Another of Eliethor's spells?" Aranok asked, scuffing his feet in the loose dirt.

Ariana nodded. "She said that she'd modified it with as many things as she could think of, so it may do a lot more than the Mechs of Arnhammen's childhood."

Ariana stayed with it and once they had moved into the new tunnel, Arnhammen stood and moved with them, the barrier cubes following him and still enclosing them.

The Mech moved methodically, digging in the direction Ariana had set, so it came as no surprise when they were attacked from behind by a group of skeletons.

"I knew it was too quiet," Aranok said, slipping his sword from its sheath and positioning himself to protect Ariana.

The skeletons charged.

The barrier made several fall apart. The skeletons ignored their companion's bones, walking straight over them.

"They're still attacking!" Erendell called to the dwarf.

"Aye, Lassie. We'd best be crunching some bones then." Arnhammen dropped the barrier spell, the light flaring brightly before going out and laid about him with his mace.

Grald contented himself with a thick-bladed sword breaker, the notches catching the bones and snapping them easily. Erendell had brought a holy dagger out from somewhere. The barbarian, dark elf and dwarf soon dealt with the threat.

Aranok put his sword away. *I didn't need to worry after all.* He felt oddly self-satisfied at the thought.

Moments later, the digger hit a stone wall and Ariana stopped it untying the leash from her wrist.

"I need to use an All-Seeing Eye spell to see what is on the other side, before I use the Mech to dig through." She sat down on the floor, away from the Mech and closed her eyes, murmuring the spell to herself.

As the others waited, Aranok's sharp ears caught strange scratching, scuffling sounds from the other side of the wall.

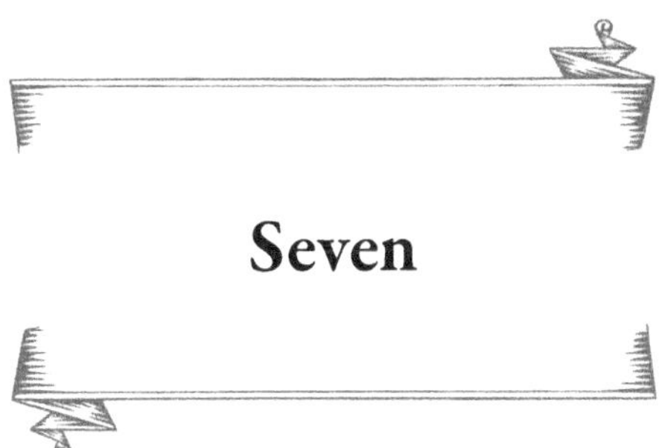

Seven

"It looks as though the Hellhounds are in place, Lord. What is keeping those adventurers?" the Jar grumbled.

Aracan Katuvana moved to the window and waved a hand over Grald's picture, then over Erendell's picture.

On Grald's picture, the pink ring became a deeper colour, almost the same colour as the Bougainvillea that grew wild in the tropical forests of the Southern Islands.

"Ah yes. An intriguing thought that, Lord," the Jar cackled.

Katuvana gestured and a green glow surrounded Erendell.

"Erendell, you will activate the digger again. Grald you will assist her by doing anything she asks you to," the Jar whispered. Both glows flickered as the instructions sank into their minds.

Katuvana went back to his throne.

"THIS IS TAKING TOO long—we need to be in and out of the Dungeon quickly!" Aranok muttered.

Ariana said nothing, still concentrating on her spell.

"We could just dig through," Erendell suggested brightly. Grald nodded in enthusiastic agreement, staring adoringly at her.

Aranok frowned at them. Grald is supposed to be a renowned warrior. Why is he acting like a love struck urchin?

"Don't be daft, Erendell. I thought you had more sense than to run into an unknown situation."

"She is not daft!" Grald's temper flared. "I agree with her. We ought to just dig through and deal with whatever comes when it happens."

"Barbarians!" Arnhammen snorted. "Always rushing in swords waving before they should."

"Because we're brave, Underdweller! We don't hide in holes like some people!"

Aranok groaned. "Grald, please be quiet and patient. Ariana is working as fast as she can."

"If she's half as powerful as my Erendell is, she'd have found out by now." Grald moved forward, his hand on the hilt of his sword-breaker.

Aranok blinked. "Your Erendell?"

"Shut up," Ariana said with her eyes closed. "I can't hear properly."

"Well, we'd hear it a lot better without that wall in the way. Help me, Grald!" Erendell shouted and rushed past the seated mage to the Digger Mech, followed closely by Grald. The dark elf crouched down and began to activate the Mech.

"Ye stupid Drow! Ye're not going to do this! I willnae let ye!" Arnhammen lunged for Erendell only to run into Grald.

"You might not want her to, but you will not stop her, I'll see to that!" the barbarian retorted and pushed the dwarf back.

A wrestling match ensued.

Aranok groaned again and tried, unsuccessfully, to push himself between Grald and Arnhammen, trying to reach his sister.

Ariana let her spell dissipate.

"What's going on?" she asked as she opened her eyes. "No," she gasped scrambling up onto her feet.

Erendell had activated the Digger Mech and while Aranok had been trying to break the wrestling match up, the Mech was already halfway through the wall.

"What do you think you're doing, Erendell?" Ariana yelled.

"Aranok said it was taking too long, so I decided to speed things up a little," the half Drow said in an unconcerned manner.

"You idiot, Erendell, there's a guard post behind the wall! They're…" The Mech broke through the last of the wall. Behind it stood four massive two headed dogs, drool dripping from between their six inch fangs as they growled at the party from atop a wooden platform.

"…waiting for us." Ariana shook her head ruefully. She deactivated the Mech with a flick of a finger and a small magic pressure before it could start to dig into the platform.

Erendell backed up quickly and bumped into Grald. The barbarian dropped Arnhammen to the floor and spun to catch the elf as she fell. Aranok jumped back to avoid being knocked over. Grald set Erendell back on her feet and moved back slightly, loosening his sword in his scabbard.

"What the…?" Aranok asked, glancing between the Hell Hound and Ariana.

"No time now, Brother, we need to get out of here!" she replied, turning to run back down the tunnel.

"Going somewhere?" a voice drawled languidly from the shadows.

Arnhammen scrambled up and hurled himself between the surprised mage and the rest of the tunnel.

Ariana produced a mage globe and lit it with a gesture. It flared bright white and lit the whole tunnel revealing a figure wearing luxurious, deep red velvet, in the form of a hooded robe, its face in hidden by the shadow.

"That's a little too bright, young human," the voice said. "Here, let me dim it for you." The figure made a motion with a gloved hand and the mage globe changed to a pale yellow light. "That's much better."

Aranok found that he couldn't move. Neither could Ariana, Erendell or Grald.

Arnhammen pulled his mace from its sling and growled, "Get ye gone from this place, Unholy One. Get ye gone in Tyr's name, lest ye taste His Wrath through mine Holy Mace!"

As the dwarf invoked Tyr's name, he struck the weapon against the floor, and it burst into deep blue flames. The figure shrank back from the mace as Arnhammen advanced on it and the hood on the robe fell back, revealing the figure's face.

Aranok gasped "Liana!"

"No, Half Human. I am the Lych Mistress, Keeper of this Dungeon that you shall soon languish in," the elven woman replied harshly. "Seize them!"

Around them ten women appeared, all dressed in skimpy tight leather outfits with high-heeled boots. They seemed to have no weapons, but their long fingernails were filed into points and their long hair was plaited and tipped with blades.

"Ye shall never take us, Unholy One, for no matter who ye be, the power of Tyr be far greater!" Arnhammen roared and charged at the Lych Mistress.

Four of the women dove on the dwarf and he bashed them away like so many flies at the end of a horse's tail. They slammed up against the walls of the tunnel, disturbing the solidifying spell so that earth crumbled around them. The women screeched, showing sharpened teeth.

Arnhammen ignored them and attacked the Lych Mistress again. This time his mace made contact and the elven woman screeched and disappeared in a flash of blue light.

The rest of the party found they could move again and, drawing their weapons, attacked the other six women. The first four attacked Arnhammen again, trying to get close enough to scratch him. He smashed two of them to the ground, caving their skulls in like melons, the pink-grey brain matter and shards of bone splashing over the dirt.

Ariana loosed fireball after fireball at the two women who attacked her. She took the first one's stomach out with a single shot and only just managed to cremate the second one, before she had her eyes scratched out. She fell back against the wall gasping and dragged a vial bearing the pale green fluid of a mana return potion from her belt pouch, downing it in one gulp.

The moment Erendell could move, she pulled out her long daggers and whirled on her assailants without thinking. The speed of her attack surprised them and two stabs later she was free enough to help Aranok, who was having problems keeping one woman at bay long enough to kill the other one.

"You always were faster than me in melee," he panted as he managed to slice the hand off his attacker and ran her through smoothly.

"Yes, but you can fight for longer; I tire too easily," Erendell snapped. "Careful!"

Her foe had slipped around her and had jumped at Aranok's back, obviously intending to take advantage of his distraction to slit his throat from behind.

Erendell sliced through the back of one shapely knee and as the woman dropped to the floor, slammed her other dagger down through the enemy's skull, the point of her dagger emerging from under the woman's chin.

Ariana joined Arnhammen to take out the last two, having recovered her breath, and between her fireballs and his mace, they managed to beat the women into the ground, where their blood turned the dirt into mud and their flesh roasted as their clothing burned.

When all of the attackers were corpses on the floor of the newly dug tunnel, the party regrouped at the entrance; Ariana collecting the Digger Mech by levitating it to her.

"Why didn't the Hell Hounds join in the fight?" Erendell asked no one in particular.

Aranok looked back up the tunnel where the Hell Hounds were still perched up on their wooden platforms, then calculated the distance between most of the corpses and the guard post. "I'd guess that they have an assigned area to guard and unless they are ordered otherwise or an enemy steps into the assigned area, they don't leave their post."

"Just as well really," Ariana wheezed. "I'm almost out of mana as it is and having those animals assail us as well would have finished me off."

"We can't take time to rest now," her brother told her gently.

"I'll be fine as soon as I can get my breath back," she smiled back at him.

"What should we be doing about this tunnel, Lady Mage?" Arnhammen asked.

"I have a magical object that should do the trick." She fished around in her bag and pulled out what looked like a grey stone brick about the size of her palm. She placed it on the ground in the centre of the tunnel entrance. "Stand back."

The rest of them pulled back until they stood against the opposite wall.

Ariana swallowed the contents of a second mana return potion, and then held her hand out over the brick. "Alta!" she commanded, and the brick began to grow rapidly. She moved back as it grew and spread out to fill the hole that they had made. It began to integrate with the stone of the walls on either side of the hole.

"Beleg!" Ariana's second command stopped the brick's growth immediately. Once it had finished, the wall looked like it had never been breached, taking on the density and colour of the surrounding stones.

"I take it you strengthened the stone as well," Erendell commented, working one of her shoulders.

Ariana nodded and looked round at her friend. "Are you hurt?"

"Concern for a Half Drow, Half Elf, all trouble?" Arnhammen spat.

"Steady on, Arnhammen." Aranok threw an annoyed look at the dwarf.

"No!" he snarled. "She caused that whole mess by not waiting for the Lady to return to tell us the result of her spell. Her and that Barbarian Lover of hers…"

"Grald is not my Lover, dwarf. He's mildly infatuated with me at best," Erendell returned without heat.

"Come to think of it, where is Grald?" Ariana looked around.

"He was there when the Freeze Spell was active. Where did he go after that?" Erendell frowned, sounding concerned.

Ariana turned back to the tunnel she had just sealed. "I sealed him up with those Hell Hounds." Her horrified voice echoed in the stone lined corridor.

"No, you didn't." Aranok soothed his distraught sister. "He disappeared when the Lych Mistress vanished."

"Are you sure?" Ariana sobbed.

"Yes, he was between Erendell and the Lych Mistress, I'm sure of it." Aranok pulled her into a hug.

Ariana cried into her brother's shoulder for a while, before she pulled away and blew her nose on a handkerchief Aranok handed her.

"Arnhammen, did your mace destroy her?" Erendell asked.

"Nay Drow, it didna. It wasna her real form, just an illusion and the power of Tyr broke the spell."

"So where did he go?" Ariana slumped to the floor, too tired to move.

"Let's rest here for a while." Aranok turned to Arnhammen. "Can you set up a barrier that will remain even if you sleep?"

"Aye Leader, I can and will." Arnhammen arranged the same four blue quartz cubes around the party, whispering a prayer to Tyr in Dwarfish as he did so.

Once he'd finished, the cubes glowed bright blue, rose up in the air to the height of the ceiling and began to tumble. The light dropped down in a glass-like barrier that resisted touch on all four sides.

"The warding barrier will destroy undead and wound evil creatures if they do touch it," he said, sitting down beside Ariana, before he pulled two vials of blue potion out of his bag and handed one to Ariana. "Drink this and ye're mana will return twice as fast while ye sleep." The dwarf swallowed the contents of the other and settled down, wrapped in his cloak.

He was asleep within a few moments.

Ariana looked at the vial, looked at Arnhammen, and sank to the floor holding the vial with uncertainty in her eyes.

"I've never seen one this colour before."

"Drink it, Ari." Erendell urged her "He might be a rude, stubborn underdweller, but he is still a cleric. I believe he is telling the truth."

Ariana looked at Aranok. He nodded silently, so she downed the contents of the vial and fell asleep. Aranok covered her with his cloak.

Erendell curled up in her cloak away from the barrier and fell into a light doze.

Aranok looked around. The barrier seems solid enough... but I can't just trust my sister's life to the magic of a stranger. He sat himself upright in the centre, drew his sword and laid it across his knees. Then he settled into his meditation, trusting his instincts to bring him out if anything untoward happened.

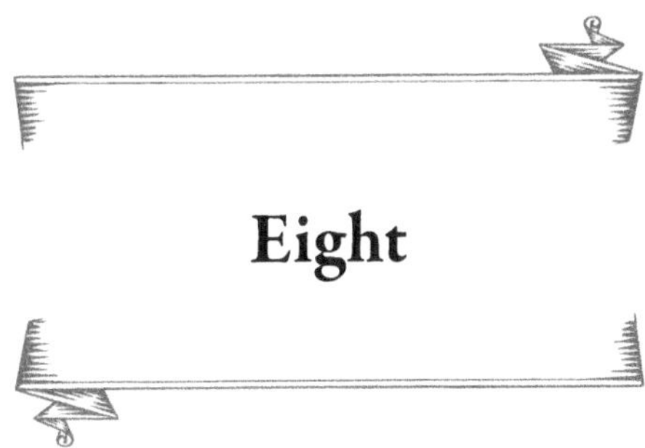

"Aww look my Lord, they fell asleep." The Jar chuckled. "Shall we have the Lych Mistress carry them away to the prison now?"

Aracan Katuvana didn't respond from his throne. The Jar squinted at its master. "My word! The overlord sleeps also. I suppose we should leave them to it then. It will be more fun to attack them when they are rested."

The glow in the Jar dimmed as its eye closed as well. Overhead the red glow dimmed slightly as the Tower fell asleep.

WHEN ARANOK CAME OUT of his meditation several hours later, the barrier was still in place. His companions all slept still, and the passageway was quiet.

That's strange, he thought. Surely with us resting, we would have been a sitting target.

He slid his sabre back into its scabbard and stood, stretching to flex the muscles that had stiffened during his mediation.

His movement alerted Erendell, who stretched like a cat and sat upright. "Still no sign of Grald?" she asked, sounding slightly anxious.

"Not concerned for him are ye?" Arnhammen said without opening his eyes.

"Yes, I am actually, as one of my companions nothing more, Nogoth."

"Don't you two start again," Aranok said sharply, hoping to head off anything unpleasant. "We had enough of that earlier."

"Yes sir, Leader, sir." The Drow bobbed her head in a subservient bow at him.

Aranok glared at Erendell, who rolled her eyes.

"Can't a girl have a little fun around here?" Aranok groaned softly.

"Okay, okay. I'll behave myself," she drawled.

"What's the plan then, Brother?"

Aranok turned to see Ariana shaking out his cloak.

"Obviously we need to find Grald, and we need to get into the centre of the Dungeon to get that crystal." He took the cloak from her and kissed her cheek as she stood up. "Are you feeling better?"

"Yes, thank you." She smiled up at him.

"There be something strange going on, Sir Aranok. Why would the Barbarian just disappear of his own accord?" Arnhammen frowned at Erendell "I still think yon Drow is up tae somethin.'"

"That's silly, Arnhammen," Ariana laughed. "Erendell and Grald were as much strangers to each other as we were to Grald. None of us had met him before Lord Harnez brought us together."

"Can we talk about this while we're moving, please?" Aranok waited only long enough for the cleric to retrieve his barrier cubes before he moved out, heading north up the tunnel. "The Lych Mistress knows we are here, so we have to move quickly."

"Agreed. Why are we going north? She'll expect us to come through the door leading to the Treasury," Ariana asked, her breath coming harshly.

Aranok slowed slightly. "Exactly. She will expect us to come that way. We're not going through the treasury door. We're going through the other one."

"But Grald said that Shilir said..." Erendell protested

"...there was a great evil behind it. Yes, I do remember that, Erendell." Aranok looked back at the dwarf bringing up the rear. "I'm pretty certain Arnhammen is strong enough to deal with something evil."

"I am honoured by ye're faith in me, Leader," Arnhammen replied.

Aranok wasn't quite sure if the dwarf was being sarcastic or not.

"It is your faith that makes you the stronger warrior in this instance, Arnhammen."

"How did the Lych Mistress know we were here and how we were planning to get into the centre of the Dungeon?" Ariana slowed a little, looking around anxiously. "Was she watching us with a spell or something?"

"Ariana, you do state the obvious sometimes!" Erendell's laughter rang off the stone walls around them.

"Shush!" Aranok said. "She might know we're here now, but I bet she doesn't know exactly where we are."

"The lady mage hae brought up a very good point though – how did the unholy bitch know? The only other people who knew we were coming here were Harnez and Shilir." Arnhammen shook his head.

"What are you suggesting?" Erendell tailed off as Aranok gave the elven signal for silence. She huffed and folded her arms under her breasts in annoyance.

"It doesn't matter how she found out; some creature may have heard the Mech digging," he said quietly. "Let's try to not give away our current position too easily."

The others nodded their agreement and fell silent as they walked.

They reached the far end of the North-South passageway. Without being asked, Ariana whispered a spell and a tiny clear mage globe formed, took off from her hand and sped around the corner.

"Ten skeletons guarding the treasury door. It's wide open," she whispered. "The further door is unguarded. They obviously don't think we'd want to go there." The globe returned to her hand, and she put it away.

The group retreated some distance down the passageway to be able to talk.

"I still think the treasury is our best bet," Erendell said.

"You always were more interested in money than anything else," Ariana said.

"I'm hurt. I do think of other things you know, friendship for one of them." Erendell placed her left hand to her heart and Aranok frowned.

"Since when did you go in for tattoos, Erendell?" he gestured at the red rose picture on her hand.

Arnhammen suddenly looked interested.

"What sort of tattoo?"

"It's nothing, just a little something I picked up on my travels." She put her hand behind her back.

"I'm not a Ranger for nothing, Erendell; I notice things. Having a full bloom rose tattooed on the back of your hand would be painful," Aranok said. "Where did you get it done?"

"Galindren. It's really none of your business, Aranok."

"What does Lady Eliethor think of it?"

Erendell stayed silent, hand behind her back.

"Ah. I see. You haven't seen your mother since it was done, have you? How long has it been since you've been home?"

"Does this really matter, Aranok?" Ariana asked. "We have more important things to do."

Aranok desisted in his questioning, but the uneasy feeling that the rose meant something significant to their quest wouldn't go away.

They decided to bash their way through the skeletons on guard, run straight past and round the far Northwest corner, where they would pause to let the kerfuffle die down. Then they would slip back to the unguarded door and go through without being spotted.

"Hopefully," Arnhammen growled, swinging his mace a few times to settle his armour's shoulder plates.

"It's better than trying to fight our way through to the centre of the Dungeon completely. Shilir tried that at the south entrance, remember?" Ariana reminded the dwarf.

"Aye, but he dinnae have a proper Mage Protector wi' him," the dwarf said. "The Guild thought this place were empty, so they nae sent one wi' him."

"Everyone ready?" Aranok asked, slipping something into his mouth.

"Yup." Erendell smiled, looking overexcited.

"Have you taken something?" Ariana asked suspiciously.

"Not much, just a little Copperleaf Candy."

"Great. Now she'll be loopy and hyper," the mage groaned to Aranok, who grinned at her.

"You should try it – livens the blood up," he replied sticking his tongue out. It was bright green.

"Not you as well…" Ariana pressed her lips together. "I thought you were staying away from copperleaf."

"Just the bread," he shrugged. "It's the berries that taste bad. I like Copperleaf itself."

Ariana rolled her eyes to the ceiling.

"When we get to the other end, I'm casting an Unremarkable spell, remember. If you're acting too crazy, it won't work."

"It will have worn off by then," Erendell giggled. "The effect of the bonbons never last long enough."

"Ne'er mind that now, can we just get on with this?" Arnhammen said.

"Lets. Get. Going!" Aranok roared out.

The party ran around the corner and along the east-west corridor. They collided with the skeletons at full pelt.

Arnhammen, who was in the lead, laid about him with his mace, opening up a path littered with inanimate, crumbled bones for the others to pass over and they kept running.

The few skeletons that chased them were dealt with swiftly and the group disappeared around the other corner. There they dropped to the floor on either side of the passageway and stayed absolutely silent and still.

Ariana whispered, "Ilya il Esgahl", pointing at each party member in turn.

They stayed there for an hour. Four patrols of skeletons walked straight past them in the first twenty minutes. When the patrols began to lighten, Ariana risked a small spell and sent her little clear mage globe aloft to scout the area. When it returned, she exhaled noisily.

"The guards are down to a set of four. If we're careful we'll be able to slip into the other door without being seen."

"You don't look happy," Aranok commented.

"I'm just tired. The Unremarkable spell saps your strength a fair bit." She pulled out a mana return vial and swallowed its contents in one gulp.

Erendell was fishing around in her bag.

"I have this." She pulled out a cloak that appeared to be made of a fine silvery silk.

"What be that, Drow?" Arnhammen massaged an ointment into his elbow, wincing as he rubbed the wound a little too hard.

"It's an Invisibility cloak, Nogoth. My mother made it for me." She looked at Aranok. "I thought that I could use it to go and disarm any traps that might be on the door or inside the complex behind it."

"Good plan. We'll follow quietly," Aranok said.

Erendell swept the cloak around her.

Until she reached the corner, she kept the hood down. Her disembodied head floated along the passage way and Aranok rolled his eyes at the grin on her face.

"Be serious," he hissed at her.

"Why? This is much more fun," she replied and skipped ahead of them.

"I thought she said the candy wore off too quickly?" Ariana grumbled.

He shrugged. "You know how Erendell is; too loopy for her own good sometimes."

"It was that which got her thrown off her Novitiate," his sister reminded him. "We have to keep her under control, or she'll ruin everything."

"I'll deal with it," Aranok soothed his sister. "I've been dealing with her since Nursery."

Once at the corner Erendell peered round it and then looked back, motioning for them to follow. When they reached her, she said, "I'll go and sort out the door. I'll signal when it's open."

Aranok nodded and blinked as her hands reappeared from inside the cloak.

Erendell swept the hood up onto her head and then pulled her hands back inside.

"Give me a slow count of twenty," she said, just a voice on the air, then the faint sound of her footfalls echoing around them was the only indication she had left.

"...eighteen, nineteen; twenty." Aranok finished counting and peered carefully around the corner. An elegantly boned, ebony hand appeared out of nowhere and gave the elven sign for All Clear.

The three of them crept down the corridor, hugging the wall and freezing every time one of the skeletons on guard at the treasury door turned their way.

The dinginess of the passageway, combined with the fact that the magic which reanimated the skeletons made them short sighted, worked in their favour and they slipped through the open door into a tiny passage.

Erendell dropped her hood and shut the door quietly. "I've scouted the whole complex. It's basically a tiny Dungeon within the larger Dungeon," she whispered.

"Is there anything in here? Traps or alarms?" Aranok asked softly, catching Erendell's unease.

"None. The door to the main Dungeon is locked, though. If we're quick, we can get through without having to fight."

"Ye show the way, Lass," Arnhammen muttered. "I'll bring up the rear." He unhooked his mace, having put it away for their surreptitious rush to the door.

Aranok took the second position and Ariana followed him, looking around nervously. Erendell left her head uncovered and they followed her disembodied head to the end of the passage, around to the left, into a tiny treasure room heaped with gold and jewels.

Erendell's eyes brightened as they entered and without really thinking, Aranok said quickly, "We'll raid the main treasury, Erendell. Leave this place alone."

She pouted as they exited the room into another corridor.

"Ariana," Aranok whispered. "Do you have another of those blocks that you used to seal the tunnel we dug?"

"Yes, but it takes time to grow."

"Can you start it off now on your hand and we'll drop it into position as soon as we are in the corridor between here and the main Dungeon?"

"Good idea, Brother." She pulled another grey block and muttered "Alta" to it. The block began to grow in her hand.

They rounded a left hand corner into a longer corridor and Erendell turned to Aranok. "The main door is just..." Her face paled and she shouted, "Look out, Arnhammen!"

Aranok and Ariana turned to see a Devil Demon standing behind the dwarf, swinging a huge glistening scythe. The creature's deep red skin contrasted with the black fur that covered its legs all the way down to bright red hooves that scorched the stone beneath them with flame.

The dwarf brought his mace up at the shout and the blade of the scythe bounced off the suddenly fiery weapon. The demon was thrown backwards and Arnhammen shouted to them, "Go, I'll deal with this monster and meet ye in the centre!"

Ariana looked helplessly at her half-brother. The block was almost too big for her to hold in both hands.

"Drop it, Ariana," Aranok told her.

"But Arnhammen…"

"I will meet ye later, Lady Mage! Just go!" the dwarf yelled and stood his ground against the Devil demon's second attack.

She dropped the block and they watched, unable to do anything.

Aranok couldn't draw his bow in the confined quarters of the corridor. He pulled out an arrow and tried to use it as a dart, the way he had in the tavern. It flew past the block, which was now chest height, past Arnhammen's head and buried itself in the demon's chest. The creature laughed as it ripped it out of its body and broke it in two with one hand.

"My Mistress knows you are coming, puny creatures. Run if you can, but I shall triumph here and destroy you later on her command!" The demon laughed as it swung the scythe again.

The wall was almost head height now, but they saw the flash of the blade, the spurt of blood and Arnhammen's head flying off to the right.

Erendell retched and Ariana paled. She kept hold of the brick spell as the Devil Demon stepped up to the wall.

"We shall meet again," it said, its bright gold eyes flaring with humour as its laughter was cut off as the block's spell completed.

"Beleg!" Ariana screamed in release. Then she collapsed sobbing into Aranok's arms.

"Ariana; Ariana, we have to go now." Aranok tugged his sister upright.

"I can't, Aranok. Arnhammen was meant to protect me, but I can't leave until I avenge his death and kill that demon." The slim mage sank down to the floor again, sorting through her bag of Holding.

"You can avenge him by helping to destroy the Dungeon." Aranok started down the corridor.

Erendell stared first at him then Ariana.

"Come on, Ariana," she said. "Aranok will leave us behind if you're not careful."

"He won't go far. The door at the other end is locked." Ariana frowned, then smiled grimly. "I saw that much when I sent my mage globe into the corridor past the skeletons."

There was a rattle at the other end of the passageway as Aranok found out that fact.

"I wondered why you took so long with that," the dark elf laughed.

"Why are you giggling at a time like this?" Aranok snapped as he stormed back to them.

"The door is locked, isn't it?" Erendell grinned at him.

"I swear that you have the strangest sense of humour, Erendell. It must be the dark elf blood." Aranok growled.

Ariana stood. "I found what I was looking for." She opened her hand to reveal a shining white gem on a blue silver chain.

"The Tear of Espilieth!" Erendell took a step back. "That's a powerful talisman; are you sure you are strong enough to control it?"

The gem's light brightened slightly, and a red flame appeared in the centre.

"That means there is evil close by," Ariana said.

"We're in a Dungeon of Doom. Of course there's evil close by!" Aranok snorted.

"The next time I see the Devil Demon, I will use this to destroy it." Ariana sounded far too calm as she fastened the chain around her wrist and Aranok frowned.

"Are you sure about this, little one?" he asked her, laying one hand on his sister's shoulder.

"Of course I am, Aranokkinadiel. I am as sure of this as I was when I took the Tear from the vault in the Mage Library. Lady Eliethor taught me well; don't worry about me." Ariana brushed her brother's hand aside in annoyance, sniffed and wiped her eyes with a handkerchief. "And I will be the Devil Demon's undoing."

"Of course you will," Erendell said as she started walking towards the door. "Well?" She stopped and looked at the half elf and his human sister and asked, "Are you coming or not? There isn't a locked door in the whole of the Heart Kingdoms that I can't open."

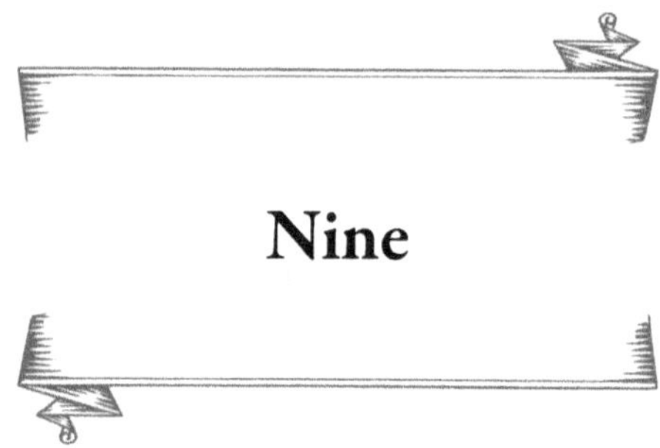

Nine

Aranok unrolled the map for Erendell.

"The treasury should be to the south. Just check what creatures are out there and come back. Don't get creative and don't steal anything yet."

Erendell unlocked the door and flung her invisibility cloak around her shoulders.

"Aranok, I swear that you are worse than my mother!"

The dark elf rolled her eyes and pulled the hood up. The door opened and closed as she slipped through.

"That's odd," Ariana blinked. "The flame just changed colour to blue. That means there is no evil nearby."

Aranok looked at her sharply. "Who was standing closest to you when the red flame appeared?"

"Erendell was. Are you suggesting that she's a double agent?"

"She is half dark elf."

"Oh, come on, Aranok. You know Eliethor as well as I do! Would she really go through all that pain and sorrow just to bring her child up as evil?"

"Eliethor wouldn't, no, but Erendell is a different story. She's changed Ariana, I can feel it."

"Paranoid!" Ariana snorted and turned her back on her brother.

Aranok sighed. My gut tells me that Erendell has turned away from good, but how do I convince Ariana of that?

"LORD KATUVANA; WAKE up, our little adventure tale has gotten more interesting," the Jar proclaimed.

Aracan Katuvana jumped and straightened. The red eyes glared at the Jar and if it had had a body, the Jar would have shrunk back at the malice in the look.

As it didn't have a body, it settled for sounding contrite as it continued, "The dwarf has been beheaded by Morian, the Valdier Dungeon's resident devil demon."

The Aracan cracked his neck by twisting his head with his hands, then rolled his shoulders. He walked over to the window showing the party's progress through the Dungeon. The ancient goblin appeared and picked the Jar up, carrying it to the stand beside the window.

"It would appear that our Sleeper agent is scouting ahead," the Jar observed as the symbol representing Erendell moved towards the Treasure Room. "Do you wish to activate her completely yet?"

Katuvana shook his head and touched the torture chamber. The Lych Mistress appeared in a panel.

"You called, oh wonderful and handsome Lord?"

"Has the Barbarian turned yet?" the Jar asked as the Aracan brought Grald's picture up below the Lych mistress. She looked down, studying the writhing barbarian.

"Not as yet. I shall employ some more... persuasive...methods. Worry not my Lord, he shall be broken."

Aracan Katuvana nodded and with a gesture closed the panel containing the Lych Mistress. He clapped his hands twice and a pair of Gremlins lifted his chair, bringing it to rest behind the figure. Enlarging the picture of Grald in the torture chamber, Katuvana seated himself.

"Time to enjoy the show, Lord," the Jar said.

"I WILL NEVER BECOME one of you!" Grald gasped, the whip slashing down and laying yet another stripe across his already raw back. He heard the whip slice down again and braced himself for more pain, but it never landed.

"Ladies, bring Sir Grald to my quarters," a soothing female voice said.

Grald frowned, trying to remember where he had heard the voice before. Four Dark Mistresses opened the fetters holding him spread-eagled to the bench. They helped him to sit up and one of them gave him a drink of water. Fear, exhaustion and pain overcame the barbarian, and he passed out.

When he came to, clean white bandages wrapped his torso, and he could feel a salve cooling the fire on his back.

He lay on his front in a large pile of silk encased cushions with a strange blue light glowing from the ceiling of the chamber. The air was cool, but not too cold and held a hint of scent to it; some kind of flower, he decided.

"Sir Grald, I feel I must apologise for the conduct of my Torturer. He was over zealous and sought to further his own ambitions by treating you harsher than I had actually ordered," the same female voice that had ordered his release said from behind him. "He has been..." the voice dropped to a seductive purr, "...punished for the impertinence."

Moving gingerly, he pulled himself into a sitting position, noting in passing that he wore clean breeches and nothing else. When he finally looked up at the owner of the voice, he recoiled. "You!"

"Sir Grald. You are a warrior of incomparable skill and intelligence. In my haste to gain you as my ally, I made the wrong decision about your treatment. Please forgive me."

"You are evil!" the barbarian growled. "You spirit me away from my friends, have my back whipped until it's raw and you want to me to forgive you?"

"I brought you here because I recognised that which your friends would never see. I recognised the longing to do something to save the world.

Grald was shocked. "How did you see that?" *I never thought it was that obvious.*

"I am a powerful mage, Sir Grald. I can see many things. I can even see your love for the Dark Elven Maiden. You can have everything you desire and more." The Lych Mistress sank gracefully onto the cushions beside him. "You can do this by joining the Aracan Katuvana's cause."

Grald moved back as she leaned toward him.

"I am no turncoat. I will not aid the destruction of the Heart Kingdoms."

The Lych mistress shook her head.

"You do not understand him. Our lord's cause is just. The Aracan Katuvana seeks to bring peace and prosperity to Quargard through rule absolute. He almost managed it before, he will complete that task this time." She laid one hand on his arm. "There is a part for you in this, if you will accept his mark."

Grald frowned. The warmth of her body subtly stroked his bare skin and the softness of her hand felt like silk against his harsher, tanned skin.

"The stories all say that Aracan Katuvana is evil."

"What is Good and Evil?" she asked him, removing her hand.

"Good is when you do things that are nice and helpful for people. Evil is when you hurt people, enjoying their pain and suffering," he answered absently, using the answer he was given as a child on the plains of Elysia. His eyes were drawn to the contours of her body under the silk robe she wore. *Is it dark red or black? He couldn't decide. There's a pattern woven into it as well... vines, I think?*

"The Aracan wishes to bring peace and prosperity to Quargard. Is that not a good motive?" The Lych Mistress clapped her hands together and a slave girl entered, translucent yellow silk bathing her fair form with golden light.

The girl carried a tray with a pitcher and two finely blown, gold tinted goblets. The girl poured out a deep red wine and handed one to Grald.

He held it carefully, admiring the colour of the wine as the second was offered to the Lych Mistress.

"But he causes pain and suffering. I know. I just experienced it."

The Lych Mistress laughed, the sound wrapping itself around his ears and rippling through his mind.

"Silly man. That was a misunderstanding. The Torture Chamber is for the sole pleasure of my Ladies of the Dark. They enjoy such treatment and draw much pleasure from it. I merely created the chamber to allow them their fun."

"Then why was I in there?" Grald sipped his wine, revelling in the warmth that it created, soothing his aches. "If I wasn't supposed to be tortured..." The Lych Mistress dropped a tiny white tablet into her wine then another into his. "What's in that tablet?" he asked, suspicious.

"Tincture of Aphrasia and a touch of Morphagia. Just a little something to take the pain away, ease your aches and relax the body." She smiled at him and ran her hand softly over the thick brown hair that covered his bare arm. "Don't worry, I'm drinking it too, it won't hurt you."

Grald shivered and swallowed his wine in one gulp.

"I won't join you," he said. I won't let her change my mind.

"You love the Viraldian girl, don't you?" she said.

He jumped as her free hand caressed his shoulder. He could feel the strength in it and a strange chill ran over his skin.

"What if I do?"

"What would you say if I said that the Aracan could guarantee she would be yours for the rest of your life?" She moved closer to him.

Grald stared at her, her lips just inches from his.

"What do you mean?"

"She is already enamoured of you. I saw that much in my crystal after we liberated you from your companions." She stared into his eyes and smiled, feeling the emotions running through him. "I can say, with complete certainty, that you would not go unrewarded for joining Lord Katuvana's cause."

"I will not hurt my friends." He moved back slightly, his breath coming faster. "And I have to complete this mission to get enough gold to free my sister."

"Aracan Katuvana can pull strings and accomplish much for the right person," the Lych Mistress replied, handing her glass back to the slave girl. "Are you in any pain now?"

Grald blinked. Whatever she had given him had relieved the pain, but had also created other, more embarrassing effects.

"I'm not in pain, but I am uncomfortable," he said.

"Let's discuss this matter later." She took the glass from his unresisting hand and set it on the girl's tray. Then she put one hand on his chest and pushed him down, her long red-brown hair surrounding his face. "I feel that we ought to deal with what is making you feel uncomfortable and get to know each other a little better first."

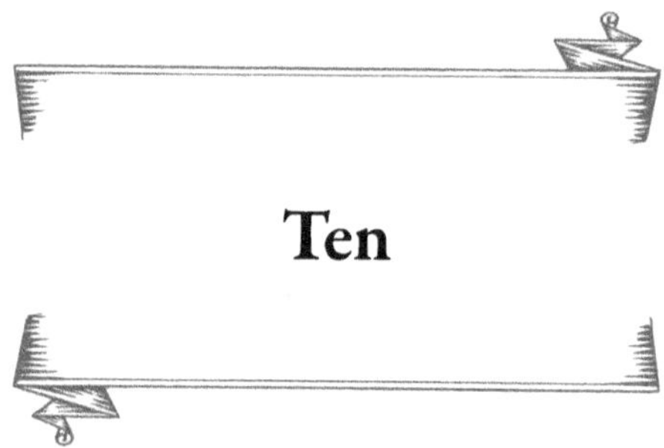

Ten

"My word, Master, that Lych Mistress is a fast worker. The barbarian will be ours soon," the Jar said with a gleeful edge to its voice.

Lord Katuvana nodded, watching the couple that writhed on the cushions with a furtive air about him. They watched for a few moments longer, then Katuvana touched an icon.

The face of a Jinranian Pleasure House Keeper appeared, the bright red rose tattoo of her rank marked on one bare shoulder, with the black thorns of a Soul-Owned wrapping around her upper arm.

"You know who calls you?" the Jar asked in an ominous tone.

"Jetara knows, Lord. Jetara will obey," the woman replied.

"Jetara, you have a Barbarian slave girl by the name of Freya in your house." The woman nodded. "Aracan Katuvana wishes you to free her and give her enough money to be able to live for several months."

"But Freya is my best girl. I can no free the child, she is gold," the woman protested.

Katuvana thrust his arm out at her and made a squeezing motion.

The Jar cackled. "You will free her, or the overlord will free you from your miserable existence!"

"Yes, oh my Master! I do as you ask! Spare me!" the woman squeaked, her hands scrabbling at the invisible fist around her scrawny throat to no avail.

The Overlord shook his hand once, then "let go". The woman rubbed her neck, panting.

"Good. See that you do," the Jar retorted, and the picture winked out.

The Overlord settled back in his chair to watch the show again...

ERENDELL FOUND IT STRANGE that the skeletons weren't patrolling the tunnel from the guard post to the treasury. She almost tripped over several dozen Gremlins that rushed back and forth carrying gold ore to the treasure room.

At least there will be no traps with this many workers around. She crept into the treasure room. It was huge, but she saw several places where they could hide from the creatures. I might as well look into the Dais room that Shilir marked on the map.

She found and disarmed an alarm trap along the next corridor and crept into the dais room behind a Troll bearing a huge stone hammer.

In the centre of the room the Crystal hung, a massive red gemstone glowing between four arms carved like dragon claws. It mesmerised her and she moved close enough to feel the breeze it created as it spun.

"Erendell." A familiar voice sounded in her head, pleasure flooding along her veins and making her gasp. "Erendell, this is the voice of your lord. Nod if you hear me."

She nodded twice.

"I am speaking directly to you to confirm that you are my favoured servant."

A burst of heat in her loins and a glance at the Tattoo on her hand confirmed the voice's veracity. The rose had gone from black to full colour, the way it had appeared when it had first been done.

"Command me, Aracan Katuvana," she replied.

"Grald has come to see the beauty of the right side and my plan for both him and you requires that the Lych Mistress bring you both to I'Mor Barad."

Erendell sighed with relief as she realised her barbarian friend was still alive.

"Bring your companions to the Heart Chamber. No one will challenge you. The Lych Mistress will bring you and Grald to the Tower and Morian will deal with the rest of them."

As the Aracan withdrew his presence from her, Erendell sighed with regret for the pleasure and hardened her heart against what she must do to her oldest friends. She turned on her heel and strode back up the corridor, noting that the Gremlins had disappeared, and the skeletons were hidden behind a new door.

ERENDELL REAPPEARED half an hour later, a wide grin on her face.

"What's cheered you up?" Aranok asked sourly.

"I beg your pardon?" the dark elf asked, one eyebrow rising in surprise.

Ariana shot an amused glance at her brother.

"Don't mind him Erendell, he just lost an argument." She dangled the glowing Tear on its chain over the map, its blue light reflecting off the pale surface of the fine parchment. "We were speculating about where the Devil Demon was now. I said that it had gone back to its little labyrinth, he thought it would be rampaging through the corridors to get to us."

"You used the Tear to divine its position on the map to prove your point?" Erendell glanced at the stone, the tiny gem now showing that little red flame in its centre.

"Yes. It even conjured a picture of the demon asleep in its den on the right place on the map." Ariana grinned, then frowned as she took in the change of colour.

Erendell giggled.

"He always did get grumpy when he lost anything. I remember the time I won his favourite wristband from him during sword practise..."

Aranok ignored his sister's stifled giggle.

"Well? Can we get to the Crystal?"

"Do you want the short answer or the long answer?"

"Have you been eating Copperleaf candy again?" Aranok rolled his eyes in disgust "Yes or no, Erendell?"

"Yes; of course. I disarmed all the traps and wedged all the connecting doors shut, so we can't be disturbed." Erendell giggled again.

"How are we getting out then?" Ariana asked.

"I've got a little something up my sleeve for that one," Aranok smiled.

"I hate it when he acts all mysterious," Erendell remarked to Ariana who laughed.

"Come on." Aranok slipped out through the door, his sword in hand.

Erendell and Ariana followed closely, Ariana wrapping the Tear's chain around her wrist, still frowning at colour of the gem.

They encountered nothing as they moved down the corridor to the Treasure Room.

It made Aranok even more suspicious, and he kept glancing down at the Tear on Ariana's wrist. The blue flame had been replaced by a red one and when he exchanged a look with Ariana, the sad look in her eyes suggested he had won their argument after all.

"It'd be a shame to leave all this wealth lying around in the wrong hands," Ariana suggested as they entered the Treasure room.

"You, greedy?" Erendell affected a shocked tone. "I never would have thought it of you, Ariana."

"I'm a high maintenance Mage! I need the finer things in life like robes and food occasionally," Ariana said, sorting through a large pile of assorted precious and semi-precious stones.

Aranok noticed that she would touch the Tear to each one as she did and only put it into her bag of holding if the Tear glowed green.

"What are you doing, Ari?"

"Making sure that they are real." The mage smiled at him. "Some of these will have been looted from the cities during the Freedom Wars. I only want real stones."

Aranok shrugged.

"Fair enough." He looked around and sheathed his sword, before he started scooping gold and silver coins into his own moneybag.

Erendell waited patiently while the two of them looted the treasure room. Aranok noticed this and frowned.

"Not taking anything, Erendell?"

"I don't need any – I took some while I was here in the cloak," she answered carelessly.

"Hmm." Aranok's suspicions increased. Erendell is never that careless. She wouldn't have taken anything until we were with her before. I'll have to confront her soon; make sure she hasn't changed sides.

Once Ariana was satisfied with her haul, they moved through the only open door to where the crystal hung in mid-air. There was a faint whining sound as it rotated slowly, and red sparkles reflected off the gilded and carved columns suspending it.

"Well, there it is. How do you propose we get it down?" Erendell asked folding her arms and looking from Mage to Ranger.

Aranok paced around the dais, examining the arms of the construction.

"There are jewels inlaid in the stone. Ari, are they magical?"

Ariana laid the Tear up against one of them.

"Yes. They link together. I can see the lines of magical force holding the four arms apart and guarding the crystal. The top set is suspending the stone."

"So, if we smash each jewel, the magic will go and we'll be able to take the crystal," her brother surmised.

The Mage nodded and Aranok brought out a pair of small hammers from his bag. He handed one to Ariana.

"Here, take this." She took the hammer and started attacking the jewels on the arm closest to her.

"That's a daring plan," Erendell said from behind them. "What makes you think you'll even be able to free the crystal, let alone escape with it?"

"We haven't got time to stand around and discuss this, Erendell. Why don't you use the hilt of your dagger to smash the jewels on one of the other arms?" Aranok replied, the effort of the task distorting his voice.

There was a sharp crack and the crystal faltered for a brief moment as Ariana cheered.

"I've smashed one! Keep going brother." She turned to look at Erendell. "Why aren't you..." her voice tailed off.

"...helping?" Erendell finished for her with a wicked smile. She stood with one arm around Grald's waist. "I've had a better offer."

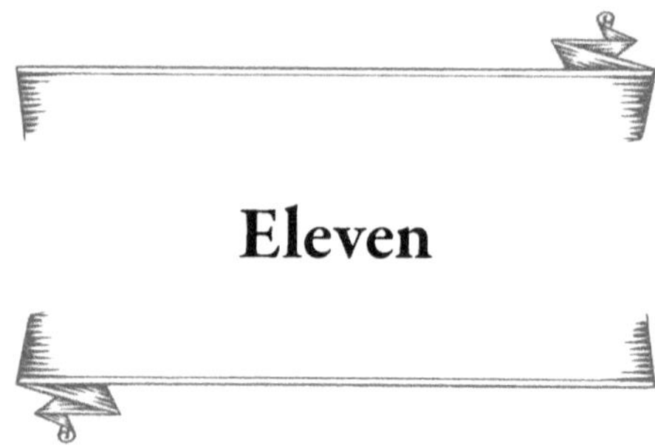

Eleven

Ariana looked around.

"Aranok, you'd better stop." Her brother didn't look up.

"Why? I've smashed two of them here."

"The young Mage is correct, Ranger Aranok," a familiar voice said. Aranok spun round, dropping the hammer and drawing his sword. "YOU!"

The Lych Mistress smiled. "Who else?"

"Erendell, Grald what are you doing?" Panic entered Ariana's voice as the two of them moved to bracket the Lych Mistress. "I thought you were our friends!"

"They still could be, young one." The Lych Mistress held out her hands towards Ariana. "Join us and you will not only gain more power than you have ever dreamed of, you will be with friends on the side of Right."

"I would never become one of the Aracan Katuvana's slaves," Ariana spat at the beautiful elf.

"We aren't slaves, Ariana." Erendell rolled her sleeve up, exposing the whole of the rose tattoo. "The coloured rose tattoo with black thorns mark us as willing converts to the right side."

"I chose to join them, Ariana. They didn't torture me while I was captive, I was treated with every courtesy and comfort." Grald smiled softly at the Lych Mistress who inclined her head in return. The hand that was around Erendell's shoulders had a red rose tattooed onto it.

"Your mother's heart will break when I tell her about this." Aranok shook his head. "And what will Liana say?"

"That stuck up bitch can say what she likes. I remember her whispering about the colour of my skin when we were children," Erendell shrieked back.

"My sister always could be arrogant. Just because she was born three minutes ahead of me," the Lych Mistress mused. "I am so glad that it will be I that inherits the throne of Alethdariel and not her; once the Aracan Katuvana's work is done of course."

Erendell and Aranok stared at the beautiful elf.

"Sister? But that would mean..." Aranok frowned, then the colour drained from his face. "Loriel?"

"Liana is my twin sister. You and Liana left me for dead after the Alethdariel raid. My dearest Lord, the Aracan Katuvana had my form brought to I'Mor Barad," the Lych Mistress laughed, her voice rolling richly around the chamber, "where Dr Cutznstix healed me, and I became more powerful than my conceited sister could ever be. I cannot die!"

"We checked you. You were dead – a stab through the lung and heart!" Aranok was distressed "Liana tried to heal you, but she couldn't."

"I lived and now unless the Heart Kingdoms bow to the power of Aracan Katuvana, I shall take great pleasure in wiping out any of his enemies – even if it is my sister." The Lych Mistress slipped one arm around each of Erendell and Grald's shoulders. "If you survive the next few minutes, give my sister my regards and tell her I will surely see her again."

The last word echoed as the three of them disappeared into thin air. Aranok turned and using the pommel of his sword hurriedly smashed the remaining gems holding the crystal.

"Hurry Ariana, we have to get the crystal and get out of here!"

Ariana nodded and attacked the gems on her arm as Aranok moved to the next.

In short order, all sixteen gems were in pieces and the crystal pulsed on the floor. Aranok wrestled it into a bag he had brought for the purpose and Ariana turned to go out through the treasure chamber.

"No! Wait. I have an item that will take us back to the entrance," Aranok cried. He began rummaging in his bag.

"Do you really think that you'll be able to escape me?" another voice said as every door leading to the dais room slammed shut, the locks clicking shut.

"It's that Devil demon again!" Ariana breathed.

"I am Morian the Wicked, Lady Ariana of Alethdariel." The creature bowed, a sardonic smile upon his face. "I am here to make sure that you never leave this Dungeon alive."

"You killed Arnhammen!" she said, her voice shrill.

"You and your companions trespassed upon my private quarters, so of course I killed the dwarf. Wouldn't you?" His golden eyes gleamed with amusement and Ariana shivered.

"Hang on Ariana, I'm almost there," Aranok said, still searching through his bag.

Ariana frowned and looked at the Tear on its chain around her wrist. She smiled.

"I'll bet you've never come up against this power before!" She thrust her arm in the air and the Tear burst into blue flame. The flame ran down her arm and around her body.

Morian laughed.

"What a pretty trick, Lady Mage; look, I can do it too."

The devil demon's eyes glowed and his body blazed with deep red flames.

Ariana concentrated on the Tear and sent balls of blue fire to crash against the creature. Morian rolled his eyes and swatted them away like so many wasps, each ball igniting the surface it landed on until the whole room was a mass of blue fire.

"I've found it, Ariana!" Aranok called, waving a red crystal on a short chain at her.

She ignored him and attacked the devil demon with lightning bolts. He deflected several, but two struck flesh and the foul stench of burning skin and fur spread through the room.

Ariana suddenly became aware that Aranok stood beside her unprotected. Without an initiating spell, she enclosed him in a protective bubble shield.

"Aranok, I have never felt such power before! This must be how a God feels!" she exulted.

"I have a transportation crystal, Ariana. You must come now!" he yelled, trying to reach through the bubble and grab her arm.

"NO! I will not give this up. I will destroy this evil creature and rid the world of its taint!" Ariana snarled. The power of the Tear pulsed through her veins and made it difficult to do anything other than react.

"You will never destroy me! I am a Devil demon of the highest Calibre, one of the Overlord's most trusted servants." The demon stepped towards her, his scythe appearing in his hands. "I destroy the enemies of the Overlord and the Dark Gods, and I do it with a smile!" The scythe blade raised high, Morian smiled at Ariana.

"Aranok! Go, use your Crystal and go!" Ariana gasped, feeling the power running through her body increase. She tried to bring it to bear on the Devil demon. "I'll vaporise him!"

"I can't leave you like this!" the Ranger replied, tears starting in his eyes.

"If you don't leave now, the backlash might kill both of us! Alone I have a chance of controlling it." The blue flame around her brightened to a white glow, so incandescent that Aranok couldn't look at her.

He backed into the door to the Treasure Room, the bubble shield moving with him. The door disintegrated as the bubble touched it and he paused on the threshold. "Ariana! I will wait for you in the Treasure Room!"

She nodded and advanced on the demon. Aranok backed into the other room, his eyes squarely on Morian.

Morian screeched as the glow touched him, but he brought his blade down anyway. It crumbled into dust in his hands.

"No! I am Morian the Wicked! I cannot die!" Ariana raised the hand with the gemstone.

"Tear of Espilieth, allow me to rid the world of this evil being." The gem flared a multitude of colours, then a broad band of white light hit Morian square in the chest.

The devil demon shrieked and where the light touched him, tiny threads of white light began to writhe over his body. From where Aranok stood, it looked like he was cracking up and where the light touched, dust floated upward.

"In the name of Espilieth, Goddess of Healing and Magic, I command you to be gone!" Another, more powerful voice overlaid Ariana's and another form surrounded her.

Is that the Goddess herself? Aranok squinted into the light surrounding his sister.

The mage's final sentence reverberated around the room, knocking dust from the dais stones and shaking the Dungeon to its foundation. Aranok found it hard to keep his feet and he clutched the transport crystal tighter.

There was a boom and a shower of ash and stone as the devil demon exploded into pieces. The dust cloud expanded, then just as suddenly contracted as it was sucked into the space in front of Ariana. All that was left of Morian was a large golden gem lying on the floor of the dais room.

Aranok rushed to his sister's side as the Goddess' presence left her and hovered in front of them. Ariana collapsed into his arms, her eyes closed and barely breathing.

"Aranokkinadiel." The amorphous Goddess coalesced into a faint image of Espilieth as he had always seen her in pictures; golden cascading hair, white pupiless eyes, and petite and curvaceous, wearing a short white and gold robe over green tunic and trousers.

"Can you do something for my sister? She's almost completely drained!" Aranok pleaded with Espilieth, the tears in his eyes overflowing. I can feel her life being consumed. He blinked and sniffed.

"Aranok…Nokkie…" Ariana coughed, and a trickle of blood dribbled down her cheek to stain the shoulder of her white robe.

"Ari, you have to rest. Try not to speak – Espilieth will heal you!" Aranok glared at the goddess, "…won't you!"

"I cannot heal Death, no one can. Ariana has given her last strength to rid the world of great evil and for that I will grant her a peaceful ending and a place at my side." Espilieth ran a hand over Ariana's face and wiped the blood from her face.

Ariana stared up at her, a gentle smile forming on her lips.

"Thank you, Espilieth." This time her voice was stronger, but Aranok could feel her heart faltering and breathing slowing.

"Do something! I don't want to lose my sister," he shouted at the deity, his pain growing.

"Nokkie, listen to me." Ariana raised one hand to stroke his face and he looked down at her. "I knew what I was doing when I summoned the power from the Tear. Only a Paladin or a cleric can channel Espilieth's power without dying. I'm not a cleric, so I knew I would die. The Goddess has given me a gift beyond price by easing my end. For my sake as well as yours." She coughed and wheezed.

"Aranokkinadiel, I must ask you to do something that will impact on the whole of Quargard, not just the Heart Kingdoms." The Goddess' voice soothed his pain, but he fought it.

"If you can't save my sister, then I will do nothing for you!" Aranok snapped.

"Nokkie, please. Do what she asks of you. If not for Quargard, then for me." Ariana grinned at him, but he was shocked by how weak her smile was. "Mother will never forgive you if you tell her that you not only let me die, but refused to do a Goddess' bidding, and I will never forgive you if you don't."

Aranok felt his sister's heartbeat stop for one long, terrifying second, then start again. He sniffed and wiped his eyes on his sleeve. Then he looked up at the Goddess.

"What do you want of me?"

"I have a loyal Cleric in Galivor. She was part of a similar expedition that claimed the lives of the whole party except her. I wish you to go to her and become her Guardian. No one, but you and I will know of your affiliation, not even Kalytia. With My Tear she is destined to be the one to destroy the evil that threatens to take over Quargard and she will need your help."

Aranok glanced down at his smiling sister and without hesitation replied, "Yes. Will you do me a favour, Lady Goddess? Allow my sister to travel with me to the sunlight outside and see the end of what she has sacrificed herself for."

Espilieth nodded and stroked Ariana's face.

"Allow me to merge with you one final time child, so that your brother may have his wish."

Ariana nodded and closed her eyes. The Goddess' form disappeared and flowed into Ariana as she took a breath. Then Ariana pushed herself up and stood, stretching slightly.

"That's better, even if it is only temporary."

She looked around at the devastation and picked up the Tigers Eye nestled in the pile of ash that had been Morian.

"This is a powerful stone, but it isn't evil. I think it might be what was there before he became a devil demon."

Aranok blinked.

"Morian wasn't always a demon?"

"No, Aranokkinadiel. Most were humans at one point. Sadly, they sacrificed their humanity to the Dark Gods and became devil demons." Espilieth's voice coming from Ariana's lips was a bit of a shock, but Aranok took it in his stride. "All that was good in their hearts became encased in stone and the gem is Morian's goodness. It would be a powerful tool in the right hands."

Ariana slipped it into her bag of holding and held her hand out.

"Allow me to use the transport crystal?"

"Of course, little one." He handed Ariana the small red crystal, wrapped his arms around her, tightly holding onto the bag with the Dungeon crystal.

Ariana focused on the crystal and whispered something to it. A red glow surrounded them and when it faded away, they were standing in bright morning sunshine, the horses cropping the grass not far away.

Aranok let Ariana go and turned to look back at the entrance. One of the doors was open and a pair of green eyes stared out of the darkness inside.

"Expose the heart crystal to sunlight quickly. It will destroy the Dungeon." Espilieth said as Ariana moved to sit under a tree, sorting through the items in her bag of holding.

Aranok nodded and opened the bag, bringing the crystal out into the sunlight. It pulsed with a deep red glow and as soon as the sunlight hit it, the red pulse weakened.

From the door there was a desperate scream and a deep rumble as the walls below them caved in. Dust billowed out of several holes that appeared in the ground which kept shaking until all of the red glows had drained away and the crystal was as clear as diamond.

He recovered it, putting it back into his bag.

"Aranok, I must go now. Take my bag of holding and do with it as you will. The items of power might be useful for you... with a little training from Eliethor." Ariana held the bag out to him and after a moment Aranok knelt beside her and took the bag, putting it beside the one holding the heart crystal.

"Sister, I will miss you so much," he said taking her hands.

"I will watch over you, Brother. Do two things for me please, Nokkie?"

"Anything."

"Give Liana my necklace; she always did like it. And propose to her. She needs you as much as you need her." Ariana giggled, then sighed and closed her eyes.

Aranok leaned down and took her emerald necklace off. Then he kissed her cheek. "Sleep well, my Arianadrialla."

"Step back, Aranokkinadiel," Espilieth commanded.

He did as he was bid, tears sliding unbidden down his cheeks.

Espilieth stepped out of Ariana, fully formed. She turned and held out her hand to Ariana.

The slim mage smiled and died peacefully, her final breath coming out almost unheard. Then her spirit sat up and took Espilieth's hand. The Goddess raised Ariana's spirit from her body as it shimmered and became a cloud of glistening bubbles.

"Farewell Ariana," Aranok choked out. "Savo hîdh nen gurth a'muinthel."

"Goodbye, Aranok," she replied and faded from sight.

"I will see you again soon, Aranokkinadiel. Remember Kalytia please," Espilieth whispered as her presence faded.

"DAMNED GODS OF LIGHT are interfering, Lord. What would you have me do to the remnant of the party?" the Lych Mistress asked from the window.

The Aracan shook his head.

"Nothing, Lady Lych. We shall allow this to pan out, as it will. Never allow it to be said that the Aracan Katuvana interferes with the battles of the Gods," the Jar replied. "We are, however, thankful that you, Erendell and our latest recruit are safely away from that mess. Farewell."

The Lych mistress looked unhappy, but she curtsied, and the picture faded.

"Two Dungeons have been cleansed, Master. I hope this isn't the start of an alarming precedent," the Jar said. "Where do you wish to extend your vision to next?"

The Aracan surveyed the map of the Heart Kingdoms then pointed at Jinran and moved a small human piece into the forest around the Jinra Dungeon on a marble game board in front of him.

"Interesting choice, Master. Do you wish to watch or control her?"

The Aracan sat down in its chair and pointed to the window...

Don't miss out!

Visit the website below and you can sign up to receive emails whenever Kira Morgana publishes a new book. There's no charge and no obligation.

https://books2read.com/r/B-A-SVI-WXCOD

BOOKS2READ

Connecting independent readers to independent writers.

Also by Kira Morgana

Terrene Empire Tales
Blossom & Kitsune: A Brief Tale of Earthquakes and Nine Tailed
Foxes
Snow & Kitsune: A Long Tale of Wild Weather and Tanuki

The Dragon Flower Saga
Hat or Tiara?

The Secret of Arking Down
The Angel's Crown
The Dragon's Pendant
The Second Door

The Tower and The Eye
A Beginning
Party at Castle Grof

Standalone
The Necklace of Harmony: A short story collection

Watch for more at tpsworld.wordpress.com.

About the Author

Kira thought she was a Teacher, until Life pointed out to her that she is actually a writer. As her Cats, Kids and Partner (in that order) approved, she decided to agree with Life.

Currently she is working on a seven book Science Fantasy series, with several accompanying spinoffs and as "A.E. Churchyard" on several Science Fiction projects.

As if that weren't enough to do, she also sings in a Chorus Line, takes Tap lessons, and is delving into the world of Illustration and Graphic Novels

She does all this from a body in South Wales, UK. Where her mind is, she hasn't yet worked out, because apart from seeing a lot of fantasy creatures, she hasn't actually managed to find someone with a connection to a map app...

Read more at tpsworld.wordpress.com.

About the Publisher

Teigr Books is the official Publisher of all Kira Morgana, A. E. Churchyard and Mandy E. Ward books.